SEXTET IN A MINOR

SEXTET IN A MINOR

A Novella and 13 Short Stories

NORMA KLEIN

St. Martin's / Marek

NEW YORK

The stories in this collection have been published in the following magazines:

"Easter Rabbits in July": *Quarry*; "The Wrong Man": *Quartet*; reprinted in *Prize Stories 1974: The O. Henry Awards*; "The Chess Game": *The Southwest Review*; "Someone's Face at the Door": *Prairie Schooner*; "The Interview": *The University of Windsor Review*; "The Gray Buick": *The University Review*; "The Missed Sunday": *The University Review*; "Sleeping Pills": *The Denver Quarterly*

SEXTET IN A MINOR: A NOVELLA AND 13 SHORT STORIES. Copyright © 1983 by Norma Klein. All rights reserved. Printed in the United States of America. No part of this book may be used or reproduced in any manner whatsoever without written permission except in the case of brief quotations embodied in critical articles or reviews. For information, address St. Martin's/Marek, 175 Fifth Avenue, New York, N.Y. 10010.

Design by Mina Greenstein

Library of Congress Cataloging in Publication Data

Klein, Norma, 1938–
   Sextet in A minor.

   A St. Martin's/Marek book.
   I. Title.
PS3561.L35S49   1983   813'.54   82-16911
ISBN 0-312-71348-7

First Edition

10 9 8 7 6 5 4 3 2 1

In memory of George P. Elliott

Contents

SEXTET IN A MINOR

SEXTET IN A MINOR

SCREW VIEWS

"Are you trying to kill us all?" Linda Tomlinson asks coolly.

The small red Maserati in which she, her husband, Stanley, and their fifteen-year-old son, Jimmy, are driving along the Italian Alps has suddenly jolted forward, heaved back, and jolted forward again. They rented the car in Europe—easier than shipping their own over—but Stanley is suspicious of it. You don't know where you stand with these damn things. They're nice-looking, all right, but God knows what they have for engines. Spaghetti carbonara, probably.

"Look, take it easy, will you?" he says. "We'll make it."

Linda laughs dryly. "Let's hope."

Her idea would have been to take trains or planes the whole way. Here you spent half the lousy trip careening over bumpy roads—for what? A view of a couple of mountains? She'd grown up in Colorado, she'd seen enough mountains to last her a lifetime. Still, Jimmy might like it. Ironically, though, they could just as easily have left Jimmy at home, which was Stanley's idea. "Why lug the kid all over Europe?"

was his reaction. "Lug? Why *lug?*" And so, out of a semantic argument arose the decision, casually, indifferently seconded by the boy himself, to make it a threesome. And, as had happened so often in the past, Linda had no idea if she really wanted it or just enjoyed opposing Stanley.

Frankly, she didn't like children. Didn't like babies—well, who did, with all the muck of diapers and formulas—but basically liked, well, adults. People over thirty. They have another son, John, three years older, who is in Montana, working on a cattle ranch. He'd fallen in love with some crazy cowgirl one summer they'd all spent out there and now went back every August to "ride the range" duo. Well, great! If he's happy.

Stanley has gotten out of the car and is standing, arms akimbo, glaring at it. Then suddenly his mood changes. "Will you *look* at that view!" he says. "Just look at it."

Linda casts a disdainful glance at a dazzling expanse of snow-capped Alps. "Screw views," she says, lighting a cigarette.

"Watch your language, Mom," says Jimmy from the backseat.

"That's right. You tell her, Jim," Stanley says. He gets back in the car. "Here your mother's such a culture bug. Beauty, beauty everywhere—but you show her some really gorgeous stuff that half the population of the world would give their eyeteeth to see and what does she say?" Before Linda has a chance to repeat what she said, he says, "I thought you gave *up* smoking."

"Well, at times of tension I indulge. Any objections?"

"Tension! What's the tension? We're gliding along an Alpine slope, we're—"

"Stanley, shut up and drive, will you?"

"Yeah, let's move, Dad," Jimmy says. Sitting in the backseat, legs up, eating a bunch of grapes, he is, in fact, as indifferent to the scenery as his mother. A withdrawn, peculiar boy, he delights in mathematical puzzles and misses the billboards of U.S. highways on which he could count letter combinations.

Stanley drives on. He is a good driver, but the road is narrow and bumpy. He drives doggedly, silent, angry.

"We should've gotten an air-conditioned car," comes from Jimmy some ten minutes later. "That's the life."

"Umm, they *are* nice," Linda says dreamily. "The Hunts had one, didn't they? That couple who both—"

Stanley slams his fist down on the steering wheel. "You two are the limit, I mean it. Air-conditioned cars! Look, here you are—in *nature*. You come out of that filthy city [he meant Paris, where they'd spent two weeks]. Enjoy it, for Christ's sake!"

"I don't like nature," Linda says, chainlighting another cigarette. "People are always saying, Nature *this*, nature *that*. As though it were some fat old lady sitting around on her butt, knitting."

"Well, nature *made* you," Stanley says grimly.

Linda guffaws. "She did? I must have been asleep."

"Jimmy, I tell you, we've got to wash your mother's mouth out with soap."

"Yeah, Mom, stop the dirty talk."

Linda blows smoke out at the Alps. "Puritans, my God! I'm in a nest of Puritans."

But she is silent for the next half hour until they reach Lake Como.

A WOMAN OF EXPERIENCE

"Here is your key," Signora Montini says, smiling genially.

"Thank you." Patrick slips it in his pocket and with his other hand takes hold of Beryl. Fingers entwined, they stroll into the dining room.

Beryl has a dread that they will be taken for ordinary honeymooners. If they are five minutes late to the dining room, she feels people will look at them with sly smiles—we know what *they've* been up to. What if they had! It isn't some gross, obvious thing of discovering the "joys of the sensual life." It's just, well, they want to and it's warm and Patrick for once doesn't have to rush off to work. We lived together three *years*, she wants to tell everyone. We know all about it. We *know*.

As for Patrick, he couldn't have cared less what people thought or did not think. He is a physicist and saves his intense thinking for his work. "What's wrong with honeymoons?" he says. "I think they're nice."

"They are nice," Beryl agrees. "I just don't want people to think I'm an innocent young thing or whatever."

"Well, anyone can tell looking at you that you're a woman of experience," Patrick says.

"They can?" Beryl says happily.

"Sure," Patrick says. "Sure they can."

STANLEY IS IN A BAD MOOD

"Who chose the damn place?" Stanley wants to know.

They have just been informed that Jimmy, whom they thought would have a single room, will have to share a room with a Mr. Carlisle, a bachelor whom Signora Montini has described as "multo sympatico."

Linda is sponging off her makeup with a pink cloth. "Look, someone—Phyllis What's-her-name—said it was the best, bar none, place on the Lakes. *And* you wanted tennis. *And* it has tennis. *And* you wanted golf nearby. *And* it has golf nearby."

"*And* I wrote in for two separate rooms."

"Okay, so it's the holiday season. They're cramped."

"They lied," Stanley says gloomily, unpacking his shaver. "They lied to me. They said in the letter—"

"Maybe they don't know English that well. They got mixed up."

"Yeah, sure."

"Anyway, what does it matter? He'll be okay."

"No, it's just I like—when I want something, it should happen. *If* I can pay for it."

Linda snorts. "I'm going to engrave that on your tombstone, Stanley. *If I can pay for it.*"

He reddens, then says quickly, "You know, Lin dear, I'd love to see you manage without some of that moola you have such contempt for." He picks up the dress on the bed. "What paid for this? An epic poem?"

"So, let him sleep in here," Linda says, dodging the issue deftly, "if the thing strikes you as so terrible. They can move a bed in."

"Well . . ."

"He'll witness such orgies it'll traumatize his soul."

Stanley hesitates. "He'll be okay where he is," he says after a moment. He plugs in the electric shaver and begins peering over Linda's head in the mirror as the bell downstairs rings for lunch.

BAGELS AND LOX ON EL AL

"I've traveled on all of them," Stanley says, "and let me tell you, El Al's got them all beat, right down the line."

"In what sense?" Beryl says. "Food?"

They are seated at one long table—Mr. Carlisle, the anonymous bachelor, Stanley and Linda, Patrick and Beryl, with Jimmy at one end. It is a simple room—long wooden tables such as might adorn a boarding school refectory. Around the room are other tables, crowded with hungry tourists—the Pensione Montini functions as a restaurant as well as a hotel. There is a pleasant buzz of noise, a delicious smell of roasted veal. Outside, through the wide glass window, lies the blue expanse of Lake Maggiore.

"Yeah, well, food, everything . . . Let me tell you something. I took El Al this winter—had to go over to Holland to see about one of our factories there—and you know what they served us for breakfast Sunday morning? Guess!" He looks at them with an expression of childlike glee.

Patrick smiles. "Bagels and lox?" he says.

"Right!" Stanley beams. "But what bagels and lox! Those bagels!"

"Flown right in from the Bronx, eh?" says Mr. Carlisle. A tall, lanky man in a yellow shirt, he has scarcely spoken until now except to reveal his profession: He is a podiatrist.

Stanley casts him a withering glance. "What do you mean? Those bagels were something special, let me tell you. I've never tasted bagels like those and I've been eating bagels for a long time. You know, Max Lerner was on the plane, right behind me he was sitting, and he got a big bang out of those bagels, too. Someone like Max Lerner, he's been eating bagels since way *way* back."

"I've always liked the Dutch airlines," Mr. Carlisle says. "If they're anything like the Dutch ships we had when I was in the service, they're pretty good."

"Noo," Stanley drawls. "Not Dutch. No, I'll take Belgian, maybe French, but not Dutch." He looks at Beryl's plate. The shank of veal lies on it half-eaten. Only one bite has been taken out of the gnocchi. "What's the matter with you? You aren't eating anything."

Beryl looks up, startled. "Well, the meals here are so huge."

"You eat like a bird, picking at everything." He looks up at the tomato salad that is about to be served. "You going to eat all of that?"

"I don't know," Beryl says. "I'll see how hungry I am." She looks up at him. "Would you like whatever I leave over?" she says in an overly polite voice.

ON THE RAFT

They lie on the raft, pressed close together, Patrick's arm around Beryl. The raft rocks gently. From where she lies Beryl can see Patrick's eye, very large, flecked with numerous colors that she's never noticed before—green and brown and even yellow.

"What a beautiful woman," she says. "Didn't you think she was?"

"She was unusual-looking," Patrick agrees. "Striking."

"She must be rich, don't you think? I mean, she had that air . . . But he was so *awful.*"

"He's a businessman," Patrick says briefly, eyes closed.

"Still . . . I wonder why her hair is white. It must be premature."

There is a sound of splashing and Beryl hears the voice of Mr. Carlisle call out, "Umm . . . This would be charming anywhere." He pokes his head up on the raft, hanging on and kicking. They both turn just barely to stare at him.

"It's getting warmer," Patrick says, clearing his throat.

Mr. Carlisle smiles vaguely and, lowering himself, swims soundlessly away.

Patrick turns to say something, but Beryl puts her hand over his mouth. "Ssh," she says, smiling mischievously.

He smiles down at her. "What? I wasn't going to say anything."

"You were going to call him back."

"No, I wasn't."

"Really?"

"Sure."

"What is a podiatrist?" Beryl says, propping herself up on her elbows. "It sounds so esoteric."

"Someone who cuts up people's bunions and that sort of thing."

"How awful!" She muses. "What a thing to be." But the thought passes quickly—feet are dull. She settles down and they lie back together, enjoying the silent communion of sunbaked bodies.

CAN THIS MARRIAGE BE SAVED?

Beryl lies quietly. Tired from swimming, she feels totally relaxed and lets Patrick caress her body, kissing her breasts, while she just lies there and thinks: How nice this is! His fingers are cool from the water and this gives a special, tingly sensation that is delightful. And it flashes through Beryl's mind that she cannot be any happier than she is now, that she is at the peak of her happiness, and this frightens her. Suddenly she thinks: I should caress him. I'm being too passive, and she remembers how Patrick once said he likes to be caressed and how this had surprised her because she hadn't thought of Patrick, basically, as someone who liked sensual things. Of course, he liked sexual relations but she had never thought he would like to be caressed. And then she thinks of articles she's read about young wives not being responsive enough, articles that end up in *The Ladies Home Journal* as "Can this Marriage be Saved?" and as though urged on by these words that she sees before her, she slips her hand over Patrick's back and slowly, as light as a feather, begins drawing her fingers along his buttocks and back.

AN EVIL CHILD

Stanley wants to get Jimmy moved to another room, away from Mr. Carlisle. They have been at the pensione one week. "I just think he might pull some funny business," he says.

"What funny business?" Linda says coolly.

"Oh, you know. Those old queers do all kinds of weirdo things."

"Such as?"

"Such as—plenty of things. Look, I know these characters. I've seen them in action."

"Where?"

He was exasperated. "What are you trying to do? He's not a queer?"

"He's a very sensitive, gentle man."

"Oh God!"

"You want to stereotype everyone. People are more complex than that."

"So—you let him rape your own son."

"Oh rape! Jesus, Stanley. I mean, even you can see Louis is hardly the type to—"

"Louis!"

"His name is Louis. Any objections?"

"I just love the way you say Loo-iss." He purses his lips, imitating her.

"What should I say—Louis?"

Stanley begins waltzing wildly around the room, embracing an invisible woman. "Meet me in Saint Louis, Lou-is, meet me—"

Linda puts the finishing touches on her hair. "You are a child, Stanley. And an evil child at that."

He turns down the corners of his mouth. "There's a new one. I ought to keep a list of these."

"I'm ready," she says, facing him.
He puts his hand on her behind. "Evil, huh?"
"Drop it."

A MORNING SWIM

Mr. Carlisle likes his morning swim. He wakes up usually around six and, moving quietly so as not to awaken Jimmy, gets into his bathing trunks and goes down to the lake. The air is slightly chilly at this time of morning, but the water, as though it has managed to contain some of the warmth of the previous day, is mild and pleasant. Mists rise from the water, partly obscuring the opposite shore, though through the mists streams the faint yellow sun of morning, creating strange effects of light and shade. As he swims, it is often hard to tell the direction toward which he is going. By now he knows the way, knows it instinctively, but the mist often drifts up right in front of him so that he can see nothing. It is a strange but pleasant feeling, swimming with a steady stroke through the clouds of mist and then suddenly discovering a clear spot and seeing the opposite shore, until then invisible, clear in all its details. The woman going to the water's edge to fetch some water for washing, the cows that are being led out of the barn, everything appears as sharply etched yet as small as the view seen in an Easter egg that has been hollowed out to create a tiny scene. He is a good swimmer. He can swim long distances and not get tired. His long arms stroke steadily but without seeming effort on his part, so that he finds he can forget entirely that he is swimming. His arms and legs seem to act independently of him. Sometimes he turns over and floats for awhile. The lake water is so smooth and still that there is no danger of being splashed by waves, and he will float for five or ten minutes, drifting wherever the water takes him, squinting up at the pale sky.

When he gets back, he feels remarkably light. The effort the swimming takes is suddenly noticeable in the lightness, almost dizziness, in his head. His skin is pale and ghostly white, the tips of his fingers are bluish. By then the sun is out, no more mists. The opposite shore stands out distinctly with every detail in place and he feels as though the mood is shattered. Yet he likes this. He likes the thought, as he strolls back to the pensione, that only he, of all those sleeping in the house, has been up to see the lake in its strange, early-morning mood. The rest—the hot sun, the intense blueness of the lake at midday—all that is beautiful but it is there for anyone to share, whereas this is his alone and for that reason he prizes it.

THE FIRST HALF AND
THE SECOND HALF

"Could I have half of the paper?" Beryl says.

They are at breakfast and Guilia, the maid, is pouring coffee from an enamel pot. The room is relatively empty and quiet.

"Which half do you want?" says Stanley.

"Oh either—the first half, I guess."

Stanley grins. "Well, here's the second." He winks at Patrick. "I always say, Women are spoiled enough . . . Never give 'em what they want."

Beryl turns red and silently takes the second half.

Later, as they are getting up, she asks in a level, quiet voice, "Could we have the first half when you're done to see the sports?"

Stanley looks at her indignantly. "No, you may not," he says. "I'm not done with it, if you don't mind."

"Stanley, it's not your paper," Linda says.

"It is so." He looks at her angrily. "I found it out on the lawn."

"Yes, but you didn't buy it."

"I think Mr. Carlisle bought it," Patrick says. "I believe the paper is his."

"Well, 'Mr. Carlisle' isn't here," Stanley says, mimicking the name, "and until he appears, this paper is mine."

With a quiet rage and satisfaction, he elaborately continues his reading, though there is, in fact, nothing further he wants to read. Naturally, Linda took whatever side he wasn't on! Naturally! Well, that's an old story, yet it rankles even now and he feels himself screened off behind the paper like a goalie hiding behind a wire fence, hiding from all of them.

PHOTOS

"I want to apologize for my husband," Linda says. She has come down to supper early because she knows Mr. Carlisle comes early, too. They are the only ones in the dining room. She picks up a fork and runs her finger along it. "It's just, he—"

The day before there was a scene in which Stanley demanded Jimmy be given a new room or Mr. Carlisle be evicted. It came to nothing since there were no other rooms available, but there was a lot of noise and confusion, tears from Signora Montini, and general bewilderment from all who witnessed it.

"Oh, I understand," Mr. Carlisle says quickly, smiling.

Does he? Looking into his serious gray eyes, Linda almost believes he does.

To Mr. Carlisle Linda is a nervous woman with lovely hands who smokes too much. Whether he guesses at the rest—the fear of suicide; the nose fixed at thirty in an attempt to feel more self-confident; the omnivorous reading of little magazines and books; the compulsion to attend cultural events at the Y every night: poetry readings, chamber music concerts, dance recitals; the analysis tried and abandoned; the dread of leaving New York for Boston, where her husband's business is to take him in the fall—whether all these things are stamped on Linda like luggage tags adhering to an old suitcase, some worn and faded, some freshly new, one cannot say. That he senses something may, perhaps, be detected in the way in which he pauses, thoughtful, frowning, before saying, "Oh, I understand."

Before him on the table is a stack of photos, which he was leafing through when she came in. "Are these yours?" Linda asks.

"Yes, well, I like wandering around snapping photos of this and that," he says.

"May I?"

He nods.

Linda leafs through the photos. The first one is of Signora Montini's mother, a white-haired old lady who is wearing the traditional black dress and white lace cap of the district. The cap stands out from her small wrinkled face like two coiled ears. She is looking down, reading to her granddaughter, a plump little girl of three who holds a big book in her hands.

"Why, it's like a Bruegel," Linda exclaims.

Mr. Carlisle smiles stiffly. "Yes, well, the costumes do add a certain . . ."

There are others: a girl at an open market, crouched behind a row of cheeses of all shapes and sizes; an old woman in a bar with rows and rows of bottles behind her, staring with a flat, melancholy face at nothing. "My God, what a face," Linda says.

"She didn't want to pose," he says, leaning toward her. "I had to convince her no harm would come of it."

There is one of the village early in the morning, showing the river winding round a bend, the trees reflected in it, one of a woman bent over washing her clothes.

"Why, these are *wonderful*," Linda says, handing them back to him. "Really."

From the hall outside comes Stanley's voice. He is talking to Jimmy. "I said you could play golf tomorrow, not today," he says. "That costs money, you know, my boy . . . Not that money's *everything*." He comes in and seats himself near Linda.

"Isn't it?" Mr. Carlisle says.

"No, it's not," Stanley says, reaching for a slice of bread. "I can tell you that from my own experience. It is not."

"He was just joking," Linda says despairingly.

Stanley looks annoyed. "Well, it's no joke," he says to Mr. Carlisle, who quietly has removed the photos from the table and put them in his pocket.

OLD-FASHIONED STANDARDS

"May I interest you in a little wine?" Mr. Carlisle says, offering the bottle. "Patrick? Beryl? How about you, Jimmy, my boy? A touch of wine?" Ever since Linda's interest in him, he has blossomed, become more talkative. They go to local art spots in the afternoon while Stanley is off playing golf. Now, standing holding the bottle, he looks debonair, a different person from a week ago.

Jimmy makes a face. "I don't drink wine," he says. "It's sour."

"Don't drink wine?" Mr. Carlisle looks amazed. "How old are you?"

"Fifteen."

"Fifteen? Why, I began drinking wine at the age of six . . . What do you mean, reaching the ripe old age of fifteen and not drinking wine?"

"That's a good boy," Stanley says. "You stick to that athlete's training." He turns to Mr. Carlisle. "You know, I'd appreciate it if you'd ask me about these things first. I happen to prefer that the boy not drink wine."

"I'd drink wine if I wanted," Jimmy says loudly. "I just don't like the taste, that's all."

"Jimmy, you're being defiant," Patrick says.

"What's defiant?" Jimmy says suspiciously.

"Defiant is talking back to your old man."

Jimmy grins. "So, I guess that's what I'm being," he says.

"Did you say you were going to Monte Carlo after this?" Beryl asks Linda.

Linda is wearing a dark red dress. Her eyes, pale, watchful, like a cat, turn to Beryl. "Yes, for a few days."

"Monte Carlo, eh?" says Mr. Carlisle. "Going to gamble away your life's savings, Jim?"

Jimmy's face breaks into a wide grin. "Yeah, I'd like to try."

Stanley frowns. "You know I don't approve of that," he says in a hurt, serious voice to Mr. Carlisle. "I don't like your talking to my boy that way. No more than I liked your offering him some wine. I believe in some sort of old-fashioned standards and I'd like to see them respected."

There is silence at the table. Mr. Carlisle smiles guiltily and glances at Linda whom he sees smiling back at him with approval, as if to say, We know what an old fool he is, and he feels consoled. "No, you're quite right," he says to Stanley. "Save those pennies."

"It's a fact," Stanley says. "You start learning to save and you start learning the meaning of life. That's a fact."

Linda bursts out laughing in her low, throaty voice. "Oh Stanley, you sound like Edgar Guest," she says.

Patrick and Beryl laugh, too.

UNDER THE COVERS

They get under the covers. "The funny thing," Beryl says, "is you can tell she's glad to listen to the Pode [this was her nickname for Mr. Carlisle] since he makes fun of her husband—or to listen to you, for that matter." She buried her face in his neck. "Sweetie, she does like you. I could tell . . . And he was horribly jealous. Remember how last night she asked you about Catholicism and he said, 'Oh, everybody knows about that.' "

Patrick laughs. "Yes."

Beryl begins kissing his ear and neck. "It's so depressing, though," she says.

"What?" Patrick says, startled at this sudden change of mood.

She smiles up at him mischievously. "That you're so attractive to women," she says. "Look at the way she liked you—you could just tell. You represent everything her husband isn't. You're reserved and intelligent and kind. You're just of a different order of humanity and the awful thing is—"

"What?"

"—that you'll just keep on becoming more and more attractive. Here women reach their peak at twenty, so I'm already on my way downhill," Beryl says, "whereas men keep on getting better till they're—"

"Stanley's age?" Patrick says teasingly.

Beryl laughs. "Yes, then they're at their very peak," she says. She grows solemn again. "But, sweetie, what if you do?"

"Do what?"

"Have millions and millions of affairs with women."

Patrick smiles. "I don't know . . . That'll be a problem for you."

Beryl punches him in the belly. "Oh—you!" she says. "I shouldn't have said anything. You'll just get a swelled head."

He presses up against her. "That's not all that's getting swelled."

She feels under the covers. "Sweetie, how strange—just during our conversation!"

"Well, you must admit lying nude in bed together is rather conducive."

She smiles. "I guess you're right."

THE SUN

"You've got a good tan, Mom," Jimmy says.

They all look at Linda. Her freckles have blurred together into a warm, rosy golden color.

"Yes, your color is very becoming," Mr. Carlisle says.

Linda smiles, pleased at the compliment. "I love the sun," she says.

"Yeah, all Mom does on vacations is lie in the sun," Jimmy says. "She never does anything else."

Everyone laughs.

"I *like* lying in the sun," Linda says.

"I know you do," replies her son, "only, I want to know, what's the *real* reason?"

Stanley's voice booms out. "That's good," he says. "Very good, Jimmy. I want to know the *real* reason, he says. How do you like that?"

HOW TALL ARE YOU?

"That boy's growing," Stanley says. "Look at him, will you?"

He, Mr. Carlisle, and Beryl are watching Jimmy and Patrick play tennis.

"How tall *is* he?" Beryl says.

He grins. "He's five-ten, five-eleven by now."

"How tall are *you?*" says Mr. Carlisle.

"I'm six-one," Stanley says, seeming to draw himself up even as he stands there.

Mr. Carlisle smiles. "I guess I've got you beat there," he says. "I'm six-two-and-a-half." He looks at them both with a pleased but frightened expression.

"Are you now, Louis?" Stanley says. "Is that so? Well, I'll tell you something. When I first saw you, I figured on you as someone who had me beat—"

"—in that particular respect," Mr. Carlisle says.

"—in that particular respect," echoes Stanley. "Yes, I'm afraid I don't feel too threatened in any other areas." He grins broadly.

"No, I don't imagine you would," Mr. Carlisle says.

"Well, you're right there. I don't. No sir," Stanley says.

TOUCHING TOES

"Oh, I'm so stiff," Linda says. "I ache all over."

Patrick and Beryl stand in front of her. "Why?" Beryl asks, smiling.

"I've been trying to touch my toes," Linda says plaintively. "I just can't do it."

"You should get those Arabian shoes," Patrick says, "the ones that turn up at the toes. Then it'd be easier."

"I'm getting old," Linda says. "That's all there is to it."

"No," Beryl says, embarrassed that Linda should say this in public. "You're not old."

"Look," Linda says. She tries to bend down again, but her fingers, outstretched, only reach to her calves.

Beryl looks down with her at the fingers and at the bright red shoes that remain out of reach on the floor. "They're pretty shoes," she says timidly, hoping this will console Linda. "Aren't they a pretty color, Patrick?"

OUR WHOLE GENERATION IS FALLING APART

Stanley feels a depressed, envious gnawing every time Patrick and Beryl disappear upstairs. Screwing the whole damn vacation away! Well, why not? What better way? Damn, he ought to marry again. Just some cute little thing, Oriental maybe—they said Orientals had something special—and just go at it hammer and tongs. In fifteen years he'd be sixty, out of it. Now he is in his prime. He looks at Linda who, as usual, is stretched out like a slab of fish on her beach chair, eyes shut.

"Everyone we know is falling apart," Linda says. When she speaks in that somnolent, even voice she reminds him of Cassandra.

"Who? Who is?"

"Joe. Miriam wrote he's having back trouble. He was in bed a month. Remember how athletic he was? Tennis, skiing. And she's got bursitis . . . Tim Myer broke his hip . . . They're all going to pot, our whole generation."

"Joe's fifty."

"So?"

"Anyhow, look at us," he says. "What's wrong with us?"

"It's a matter of time," she says indifferently.

Stanley whacks his hand on his leg. "Jesus, Linda, I hate that depressing talk."

Her eyes blink open. She sees him solid, stocky, with his visorlike sunglasses. "But you look *great,* Stanley," she says, but with that hint of mockery that prevents him from feeling totally satisfied. "*You* don't have to worry."

"I *am* in good shape," he announces, pulling himself up. "What's age got to do with it? It's heredity. My grandfather lived to be ninety-two, did you know that?"

"And mine lived to be a hundred and two," Mr. Carlisle says, coming by with a sly smile.

Linda laughs. Mr. Carlisle continues down the hill.

"That guy gives me a pain," Stanley says. He rubs his nose. "A royal pain right where I sit down."

DIRTY UNDERWEAR

Mr. Carlisle opens the door to the lounge. The lights are off, but at one end he sees Beryl, wrapped in a blanket, reading, and Patrick, sitting opposite her, making some notes on a pad. He pauses at the threshold, not knowing whether he should disturb them or not. Beryl, hearing him, looks up. He smiles awkwardly. "What are you reading?" he says, still not moving from the doorway.

Beryl holds up the cover of her book; then, as though realizing he is too far away to see it, says, "*The Ambassadors: James.*"

He smiles, as though she has mentioned a person he knows and likes. "Is it the first time you've read it?"

She nods.

"Oh, I envy you. Where are you up to?"

"Strether has just met Madame de Vionnet."

"At the party? Oh yes." He stands there, smiling in a kind of daze. "How do you like it?"

Beryl considers this. "Well, I do like it—yes, I mean, I have doubts . . . I don't know. I mean, everything's so repressed and ambiguous."

"Well, of course," Mr. Carlisle says, "but that is James."

"Oh, I know it is," Beryl says impatiently (she was a Comparative Lit major in college: Is he questioning her credentials?). "His social values are so terrible," she says, staring right at him as though this is a personal accusation. "He's so petty and snobbish—I hate that!" As Mr. Carlisle says nothing, she goes on in a rush, "You feel he must have been such an awful person—with dirty underwear or something." She laughs.

Mr. Carlisle frowns and looks uncertain. This particular criticism seems to strike him as out of place, but instead of answering, he stands a moment in silence and then says, "Well, see you both at dinner, I trust," and quietly closes the door.

After he has left, Patrick looks up at Beryl and shakes his head. "What was that all about?" he says.

"Oh nothing." She smiles. "It's just he's so horribly like

this man in the book, this gossipy sort of overly intellectual old-maidish person."

"I thought you said a second ago you liked Strether."

"Oh, I do—in a book."

"But not in life?"

"Sort of . . . I mean, the thing is, in a book you know all his thoughts and so he seems more interesting, but with people, just regular people you meet, you don't know—and so they seem one-sided and dull."

"Until you find out?"

"But usually you never do. That's the thing." She gets up and goes over to Patrick and puts her arms around his neck. They kiss.

STANLEY IS IN A GOOD MOOD

Stanley stands at the door of the pensione, looking down at the lake. As Beryl rises out of the water, the bottom half of her bikini is dragged down by a pocket of lake water, revealing most of her buttocks. She pulls it up nervously and ascends the stairs the rest of the way.

Stanley is feeling good. The golf has gone well that afternoon. It seemed as though that one stroke that was bothering him for the earlier part of the week suddenly fit into place. It began to work and, best of all, to work just at the moment when he was in a tight spot and needed something, just some little thing, to get him up and beyond. It's psychological, partly—he never ignores the role of psychology in sports. If you can make your opponent feel that one small edge over him is secure, it makes it that much harder for him ever to overtake you. And by some further bit of luck, just as he made that stroke that clinched the game, Amati, the man he was meeting later about the plastics deal, happened by with a friend—they'd finished their round earlier—and saw the shot.

He heard Amati's long, low whistle as the ball grazed over the grass and then fell neatly, sharply into the hole. Amati said something in Italian that Stanley didn't follow, but a minute later he came over, shook Stanley's hand, and said, "I'd like you to meet Signore Fallagio," and Fallagio smiled and said in perfect English—with an English accent, of course, like all Europeans—"Quite a shot you just made there." Then the three of them went back to the patio that overlooked the green and had a really fine martini made with that special Italian vermouth that was just dry enough. Probably it wasn't so much the drink—the drink was fine, one couldn't deny that—but as well as the drink, it was that sense of being in really top physical condition, tired, but tired in a good way so that all your nerves were limp as a rag. It is at such moments Stanley always feels most ready and able to work. His mind seems to work for two—and he could tell right off that Amati and Fallagio are the kind of men he enjoys working with, the kind who'll be ready to get down to business when it's necessary and yet who didn't scorn and knew how to appreciate a little fun on the side. "Let me show you a little of our city you never see on your own," Amati said as they separated for dinner. "I'll drive around at nine, okay?" he added with a grin, taking the delight Italians seem to feel when using any scrap of American slang—and Stanley, playing along with him, winked and said, "Okay," imitating the Italian intonation of his friend.

Back at the pensione he finds Linda is out, which is all to the good. No need to shatter his good mood yet. He takes a really scalding shower, the kind that turns your skin bright red and makes you feel that every muscle in your body is dissolving, and then he turns it on cold, as cold as he can stand, so cold he gives out yells and war whoops and goes splashing around in the shower, laughing aloud from pleasure. Then a brisk rubdown with the towels—though they weren't the kind of rough, heavy towels they had at the club in New York, but still, you can't have everything—and then fresh clothes and God, he feels good. He can't remember when he's felt so good in the last month.

Jimmy is playing tennis and Stanley watches him with a feeling of pride. He's getting that backhand—yes, he had it in him. I couldn't have gotten that backhand at his age, Stanley thinks. Look at him move. The sun is still bright over the lake, but the air is cooling off as it always does in the mountains. Stanley sighs and goes into the small side room. Signora Montini, as usual, has laid out her supply of liquors, but there isn't much—some sweet vermouth, a drop of vodka— that had been Beryl and Patrick's contribution—and some amontillado. Stanley stands poised over the drinks, frowning. Damn it, he should have gotten some Scotch. He could've picked up a bottle at that little store near the club.

At this moment Mr. Carlisle comes bounding into the room, a bottle-shaped package under his arm. Stanley looks up.

"Just what the doctor ordered," Mr. Carlisle says. "How about a little gin? Is gin what we need here?"

"Oh—gin." Stanley looks disgusted. He should have known. "Nobody got a little Scotch around here?" he says.

"How about a gin and tonic?" Mr. Carlisle says, opening some tonic for himself. "Can I interest you?"

Stanley shrugs. "Oh hell, guess I might as well. Can't hurt."

He is sitting there, nursing his drink, going over the game again in his mind, when Patrick and Beryl come up from the lake. They are dripping wet, with towels wrapped around them. Beryl has a towel wrapped around her shoulders so that when she first comes in it looks to Stanley as though she is wearing nothing but the bottom half of her bikini.

"Aha!" Patrick says. "What do I see? Gin!"

Mr. Carlisle bows. "Courtesy of—"

"Oh, what a terrific idea," Beryl says. "Make me one, will you, sweetie? Not too strong."

CHEEK TO CHEEK

A few minutes later they are all sitting in a convivial circle, drinking. Stanley pulls a bag of peanuts out of his pocket. "Like some peanuts?" he says, offering them around.

Patrick shakes his head, but Beryl reaches out her hand, into which Stanley pours a generous handful. She begins eating the nuts meditatively, licking off the salt first.

"I love Spanish peanuts," Stanley says vehemently.

"Are they Spanish?"

He stands up and looks over the records. "This certainly isn't the latest in—well, here's one. Here's an oldie. Remember 'Dancing in the Dark'?"

Beryl shakes her head. "No, I don't believe I've heard of that," she says.

"Oh well, no matter." He goes over to Beryl. "How about it—care to?"

Beryl frowns. "I'm all wet," she says.

Stanley smiles. "You look okay."

"I can't dance," Beryl says. "Not at all."

"So, you don't have to dance. Just follow. Come on." He pulls her to her feet. They begin dancing. Patrick settles down on the couch beside Mr. Carlisle. "There doesn't seem to be much for us, does there?" he says.

Mr. Carlisle smiles. "No, we'll just have to wait our turn, I guess . . . unless Mrs. Tomlinson . . ."

"Yes, where is Linda?" Patrick says.

"I don't know. She disappeared sometime this afternoon. Said she was taking a walk."

Beryl and Stanley, dancing, each hear this conversation and interpret it differently. Beryl suddenly becomes frightened. She imagines something has happened to Linda. She's done something to herself, she's committed suicide, she thinks. She imagines Linda drowning herself in the lake, like Virginia Woolf, walking inexorably into the waves and being caught up in a deep current, and later her long pale hair streaming over the water, her eyes staring upward, like the last scene of "Symphonie Pastorale." "Oh, how awful," she murmurs aloud.

Stanley looks at her. "You're doing okay," he says. "You're not so awful. I'd say you catch on pretty well."

He has the feeling Linda has just decided to go off by herself to give him a scare. It's happened before. Once she even took a train and rode all day and half of one night before she got scared and phoned him where she was. And he was up all night, worrying the hell out of himself. Well, not again. He'd had enough of threats to know the difference between them and the real thing. Linda is a threatener. She'll threaten, but in the end—and she knows this as well as he—she'll be too scared to do anything. All he hopes is that she doesn't come back worn out and tired and in some crazy, keyed-up, half-hysterical state so that he'll be up all night giving her pills, standing by her bed. And, anyway, he is enjoying himself. The gin and tonic hadn't mixed badly with the martini; it had just given him a curiously light-headed feeling, as though his feet were way below his head, so far below he can scarcely see or feel them, but it's a strangely pleasant feeling for dancing. He feels as though his feet will just go on of their own accord, lightly weaving in and out, no matter what. And he likes the feeling of Beryl's slender bare back beneath his hand, likes the fact that there is just that expanse of bare skin, reaching all the way down to her bikini and farther. He suddenly has a vision of her getting out of the lake, and he tightens his hold on her.

LINDA UNDROWNED

Linda is not found in the lake, her white hair streaming behind her, her eyes glazed with knowledge of the mysteries of death and sorrow. She is found in the dining room in a green linen dress, eating half a cantaloupe and reading Constanze. Seeing them all, she smiles. "I heard the music," she says. "What fun! Were you all dancing?"

"A little," says Beryl, slightly self-conscious. Is Linda the type who would mind that you had danced with her husband while in a wet bikini?

"We had a *great* time," says Stanley, tackling the cantaloupe. "*Great.*" He is pleased to see Linda looking so fresh and even-tempered.

"Where *were* you?" Patrick says. "We were all worried."

"Were you?" She looks surprised. After a moment she says, "Oh, I was just walking . . . I took a walk."

"The air around here is great," Stanley says. "They ought to bottle it."

"Yes, it's very pure," Linda says. She seems dreamy and abstracted. "I'm sorry you all worried about me."

AN UNCIVIL BEAST

"Oh, that man is such an uncivil beast," Beryl says, getting out of her dress. "Really."

Patrick smiles. "You're probably just attracted to him," he says, "or you wouldn't be so vehement."

Beryl whirls around, furious. "Patrick, how can you *say* such a disgusting thing? That's *horrible*. I mean, what can you think of me to think I'd be attracted to someone like that?"

"What do you mean?" Patrick says mildly. "What's wrong with old Stanley? He dances well, doesn't he? You seemed to enjoy that."

"Well, dancing!" Beryl tosses off her last remnant of clothing. "That's just the point. He's just a typical, coarse, greasy man. He looks like some kind of Italian gangster, some member of the Mafia. Of *course* he dances well. It just fits in with the rest of him." Naked and angry, she glares at Patrick. She is pink from sunburn on her collarbone and upper legs.

He kisses one nipple. "Too bad there isn't time," he says.

She flings herself at him. "Oh Patrick!" she says.

"What, sweetheart?" Patrick strokes the damp hair at the nape of her neck.

"You're so superior to—men in general."

"Well, of course," Patrick says, "that's why you married me." He steps away.

"What's wrong?" She looks hurt. "Am I—"

"On the contrary. It's just, if we want to go to that movie—"

"Oh, of course." Hurriedly she pulls on her robe and goes to take a bath.

INSOMNIA

Linda has insomnia. It is two A.M. Stanley is off touring some local night spots with his cronies. He asked her if she wanted to come, but she declined, saying she was tired, which was true. But despite two secobarbs and a hot bath, she is still up, after three hours of tossing and turning.

Mr. Carlisle sees her from the garden, standing at her window. "There's a full moon!" he calls up.

"Is there?" She turns. "I can't see it."

"Behind that tree." He hesitates."You can see it better down here."

Linda stands with her hands on the balcony railing. "Is it cold?"

"Not especially."

"I'll be down in a minute."

They walk along the lake. It is stagey—a silver expanse, the full moon. Linda is dreamy and half groggy from the pills. She scarcely listens as Mr. Carlisle talks about a variety of things—a sister, now dead, a musician. She hears the sound of his voice and catches occasional fragments, murmurs sympathetic assents to what she has no idea.

"Where is Stanley?"

"Oh, off somewhere." She smiles at him.

He smiles. Then he clears his throat nervously. "It *is* a lovely night."

"Yes."

If he showed the slightest inclination, Linda would, without a moment's hesitation, strip and make love with him, to him, right there on the water's edge, although it would have meant getting mud on her white pique shift for which Stanley, via a charge plate at Bonwits, paid two hundred and sixty-five dollars. But Mr. Carlisle is looking around uneasily. He says, "You ought to be getting back."

He wants to get back. Sensing this, not wanting him to feel put to the test, Linda says quickly, "Yes, I'd better."

At the door he says, "I'm glad you came down."

"I am too."

Stanley is still not back. Three pills is too many. Linda tosses till dawn while Mr. Carlisle walks by the lake.

MR. CARLISLE COMMITS A MURDER

No one appears for breakfast. Stanley comes home late from the night spots, Linda is begrogged by pills, Beryl and Patrick decide the hell with it, and Mr. Carlisle is not hungry. As a result they all gather with unusual promptness for lunch. It is the middle of the meal. Mr. Carlisle is speaking.

"When we were in the service," he says, "one of those

Arab boys once stole into camp. They used to steal American goods, you know, and one of them stole our camp blanket." He pauses a moment. "I took out a gun and shot him right then and there."

Linda stares at him. "What?" she says with an expression of utter horror on her face. "Are you joking?"

His face takes on a strange, uncertain expression. "No," he says loudly. "We had our duties. I felt I—"

"No, you couldn't have shot him," Linda says, jumping up. There are tears in her eyes. "You couldn't have."

"Well, it was part of our—" Mr. Carlisle stares at her miserably. He has only told the story for her sake, wanting her to see that he, too, is capable of a masculine exploit such as would have been admired by Stanley, but the effect is the opposite of what he intended.

Linda is seized by a wave of terror. "I can't believe you did that," she says and her voice is unnaturally loud and shrill. "I can't believe it. You couldn't have killed him. You—" She rises and rushes from the dining room in the midst of the meal.

Mr. Carlisle looks at them all anxiously, like a middle-aged woman caught shoplifting. "I'm terribly sorry," he begins, but Stanley interrupts him with a casual wave of one hand.

"Nerves," he says. "It's just nerves."

"You see, we were deliberately instructed—" Mr. Carlisle says.

Stanley refills his glass, scarcely able to conceal his pleasure at the discomfiture of "the rival." "Louis, find me a man who understands women and I'll give him the grand prix of whatever you like . . . Sure, you shot him. You *had* to. Military orders. *We* understand that."

Beryl and Patrick nod in unison.

"I had to," Mr. Carlisle says thoughtfully, immeasurably relieved.

Stanley gulps down his wine. "I don't know what the Israelis do with women in their army," he says, sopping up his meat juice with a slab of white bread. "Can you imagine Linda as commander-in-chief?"

"I guess they're not *like* Linda," Patrick says dryly.

Stanley grins. "I guess not."

But Linda cannot forgive Mr. Carlisle the one act of "masculinity" of which he has been capable in his forty-one years on the face of the earth. She feels betrayed. He is like all the others—cruel, unjust, a sadist at heart. At night in fitful dreams she relives the scene he has described so fleetingly, sees the dead boy, the corpse. Stanley, who has been pleased by her relative calm in the first portion of the trip, becomes uneasy as the familiar vials of pills are more readily resorted to, the blank stares flashed from nowhere in the midst of everyday tasks—opening a purse, reading a letter.

As for Mr. Carlisle, he is bewildered. Somehow, inadvertently—he hardly understood it even afterward—he has blundered. It has happened too often for him to feel surprised. But in this case he has been the direct cause. He feels like a driver discovering on the road the mauled body of some animal he never knew was there.

CLIMBING A MOUNTAIN

"Let's go to the top," Patrick says. "It's a fantastic view." Beryl is off shopping in town. The afternoon stretches ahead like an infinite roll of golden string.

"Good idea," Stanley says.

Linda looks frightened. "Oh, I don't know," she says. "I might just stay here." Since the incident with Mr. Carlisle, she has done nothing but lie in the sun day after day.

"No, come on," Patrick says firmly, taking her by the arm.

She laughs nervously. "No, really, I hate heights," she says. "It's silly, but I just have this terror of them. I can't—"

"It's true," Stanley says gloomily, seeing that another expedition will have to be put off for Linda's sake. "She can't even take a plane."

"Well, look, let's talk about it on our way up," Patrick says. He smiles at Linda. "You don't even have to look down if you don't want," he says. "Just walk up with us." He turns to Stanley. "Agreed? Linda will not look down, even if she wants, even if she begs us on her hands and knees to have a look at the view, we won't let her, okay?"

"Agreed," Stanley says.

"Well, I don't know." Linda's eyes, fixed on Patrick, are frightened and tempted. "Do you think—"

"I do think—definitely," Patrick says. He takes Linda's arm and pulls her. "Come on, on your feet. Look, here you're so worried about calories and along comes a chance to burn up about five hundred of them and what do you do?"

Linda laughs and, without even realizing it, starts walking beside him.

Patrick guides Linda up over the path. Although it is midday, the trees hanging over the path block out all the sun. It is totally silent except for vague rustlings in the underbrush.

"What's that?" Linda whirls around, hearing a sound in the leaves.

"Probably some rabbit," Patrick says imperturbably, "who's a damn sight more scared at having three people traipsing through his domain than you are at hearing him scurry away." He lets Linda cling to his arm and helps her step over a log. Gradually they emerge into the clearing. The sun is burning hot and before them spreads a wide meadow, spotted with flowers of bright gold and blue.

Linda looks out over the meadow. "It is beautiful," she says.

"That's nothing compared to what's coming," Patrick says, "but remember, you can't see, you promised."

She smiles. Somehow, little by little, her feelings of fear

begin dropping away. Patrick begins telling a long story about one of his college roommates who suffered from acrophobia and Linda becomes so absorbed in the story that she forgets entirely that they are climbing a mountain. Patrick's slow, methodical voice, the warm, steady pressure of his arm on hers has a soothing effect.

"This guy really had a problem," Patrick was saying. "He couldn't take buses or cars, was afraid to take long trips by himself—"

"Sounds like me," Linda says, laughing gaily.

"Oh no," Patrick says. "Nothing like you. Maybe a trace of the same symptoms exist in you, but nothing like the same severity. God, if you had told that guy he could have your fears in the degree you have them, he would have been the happiest man on earth. He would have paid a million dollars."

"Would he really?" Linda says, drinking all this in gratefully.

"Oh, without any question," Patrick says. "I mean, you have to realize—you have insight into your problems, which is half of the battle. He didn't even—" He waves his arm to indicate something, but Linda, losing his arm, loses balance, and stumbles forward. Quickly he catches her again. "Hey, steady," he says. "What is this?" He turns to Stanley who is marching steadfastly behind them. "Look at that. She's rushing ahead of us. First you can't get her to go, then you can't hold her back."

They are near the top now and already the air is cooler, though the sun shines just as brightly. "Right around this corner," Patrick says, and in a moment, there they are. Almost without expecting it, the clearing opens up to a wide expanse that stretches for miles. From where they stand all the neighboring ranges of mountains can be seen, extending into the distance in different shades of blue and gray. The farthest ones are misty and snow-covered, but one is so close that they can see the trees on it and the charred brown places where fires have destroyed part of the forest.

"Look, there's a little house," Linda says, pointing. "Do you see? I wonder who lives there."

Standing there, firmly, with Stanley on one side of her and Patrick on the other, she feels exhilarated, excited, as though she had just done something remarkable and wonderful, as though the mountain she has climbed is not a small foothill of the Alps, but the Himalayas themselves. The sun shines straight into her eyes so that she has to squint, and through the squint all the mountains take on multicolored hues, half hidden by the shadow cast by the spokes of her eyelashes. "It's beautiful," she says. "No, it really is."

For days Stanley can't get over it. He looks at Patrick in an entirely different light. As they are coming down and Linda has gone on ahead, wanting to try going by herself, he leans over and whispers, "You know, that's the first time in fifteen years she's climbed anything."

"Yeah, I'm glad," Patrick says and he does, in fact, feel happy for Linda's sake and for his own.

"That's the first time in fifteen years," Stanley says, shaking his head, as though he still can't believe it.

PATRICK THINKS ABOUT LINDA

Linda is curious to Patrick. Everything about her is out of a slightly different world than the one he knows personally. Her pale, silvery hair, her husky voice, and the way she lies in the sun all day; even her nervousness, the way she flares up at arguments, the quick gestures of her red-nailed hands, her sense of drifting through life—all this suggests to him an aura of wealth. Patrick's family was poor—he grew up on the South Side of Boston—and no one he knew ever had time to drift, or if they did, it was considered a family disgrace. And he himself has been working as long as he can remember, either at the store to help his father after school, at college as a waiter, or in the summer on construction crews. He has never had time to develop a sense of languid enjoyment of life, and though she comes from a different background, neither, he feels, has Beryl.

SOME OF MY BEST FRIENDS ARE ACTRESSES

"So, what're you going to do in Monte Carlo, Jimmy?" Mr. Carlisle says.

Jimmy shrugs his shoulders. "Well, my father said there're these actresses there in some film we might meet."

"Actresses?" Mr. Carlisle raises his eyebrows. "You like actresses, hmm?"

Jimmy turns red. "Well, I thought it might be nice to meet some. You know . . ."

"Certainly," Mr. Carlisle says. "It certainly would."

"Some of my best friends are actresses. That's what you're supposed to say, Jimmy," Patrick says.

"Some of my best friends are actresses," Jimmy says, grinning.

"And some of my worst enemies are actors," Mr. Carlisle says. "That's the other half of it."

SOMETHING TO SINK YOUR TEETH INTO

"She's an attractive woman," Stanley says, smiling at Patrick. "Look at those legs. I love those heavy peasant legs. Gives you something to sink your teeth into, you know?"

Patrick follows Stanley's gaze, which is directed on the stout—to him—Signora Montini who is bent over picking peas in her garden. She is squatting so that her skirt, turned up, shows round calves and strong, sturdy feet. Patrick cannot conceive how any man married to Linda can find this woman attractive. He clears his throat and scratches his chin self-consciously. "Yes, she is very . . ." His voice trails away.

PATRICK AND LINDA DO NOT SWIM IN THE NUDE

The lake is cool after the few days of rain. They swim quickly, splashing out to the raft and then back again. Patrick feels a desire to tire himself out. He swims ferociously, diving deep down and seeing how long he can stay under until his lungs feel as though they are giving way. Leaving Linda to rest on the raft, he heads out for the opposite shore, goes halfway, and then does a steady, hard crawl back, stroking evenly, one arm over the other.

"God, the water's beautiful," he says as, puffing, he hoists himself onto the raft.

"Isn't it?" Linda, stretched out on her back, smiles languidly. "I'd love to get up really early," she says, "and go in then. It must be deserted."

Patrick settles down beside her, also on his back, putting his arm over his eyes to shield them from the sun. "Mr. Carlisle does," he says.

"Really? How do you know?"

"I see him. Sometimes I get up early to work and I've seen him swimming. You know how in the lounge you can look over the lake?"

"Funny. He would." Linda squints at the bright sun, which just that moment edges toward a row of small, fluffy gray clouds. "It would be nice swimming in the nude all by oneself," she says. "Have you ever done it?"

Through closed eyes, he considered it. "I don't remember. Maybe in camp, years ago."

"It's the most wonderful feeling," Linda says. "You feel as though the water were just flowing through you."

They both lie there, contemplating this image for several moments. Patrick finds himself imagining Linda swimming in the nude and pictures her body, lean and angular, with pointed, girlish breasts. For one instant he glances over at her—her eyes are closed—and there flashes through his mind lying on top of her, being inside her, right at that instant, how warm and soft she would be inside, and then the next instant the image fades and guiltily he closes his eyes again. Linda is thinking of a time, long ago, when she and Stanley had gone swimming in the nude. It was at some place in Hawaii, at the time when she still occasionally used to accompany him on his business trips. They found a deserted edge of beach and, on Stanley's insistence, swam in the nude. He was in high spirits, splashing her, giving out loud whoops of delight, and the sight of him running up and down the beach struck her as so funny that she burst out laughing and got a terrible ache in her side from laughing too much and too hard. Even now, remembering it, she gives a brief laugh.

Patrick sits up. "What's so funny?"

She smiles enigmatically. "I just thought of something," she says.

He laughs. "La Belle Dame Sans Merci," he says. "That's you."

She feels flattered. "In what way?"

"Just this air you have." He waves his hand in an imitation of her and says, mimicking her deep voice, "I just thought of something."

"I did, though." She too stands up and prepares to go down the ladder into the water again.

"I'm sure you did. That's the point." He stares at her a

second. "When did your hair go white?" he says abruptly.

Unthinking, she touches her hair. "My hair? Oh, years ago—I was nineteen, if you can imagine it. White at nineteen. It killed me at the time."

He studies her. "It's becoming, though, in a sense. It suits you. I can't imagine you with any other kind of hair."

She pauses on her way down the steps. "I was always a blonde. It's not that different." She looks at him and smiles a little sadly. "Anyway, it's the excuse I've always given to myself for feeling old—which I have, since I was sixteen or younger."

"Oh well . . . Everyone has that. I did, anyway."

"Did you? I guess so, but it's a matter of degree."

HAVING A GOOD TIME

As Patrick bends down to light Linda's cigarette, Beryl sees, in the tension of their bodies, in their faces that are grave and preoccupied, something that has not necessarily happened but could happen. And that *could happen* comes like a chill, dazing her.

It is the last evening for most of them. After dinner everyone is going to the outdoor concert being given in a nearby town. This is the highlight of the summer season—a touring orchestra from Rome. They will stay the weekend and play three programs, one of them a repeat of the first.

"Having a good time, Louis?" Stanley booms.

Mr. Carlisle looks up, startled, from a reverie. "What?" he says in the vague, unaware voice he uses when he is startled.

"I said, having a good time here, Louis?" Stanley says again. "Enjoying yourself, huh?"

"Yes, I've been having a . . . relaxing time," Mr. Carlisle says.

"Going to the concert tomorrow afternoon?"

"No, I believe I'll set off after lunch actually."

"Oh. Why's that?"

"Well, I thought I'd just drive to the Riviera, have a look around, and then set off for Paris."

Stanley grins. "Hey, you can't fool us, Louis. Got some nice little girl waiting for you back in Paris, have you? Open the door and there'll she'll be, huh?"

Mr. Carlisle smiles. "No, I'm afraid not," he says. He raises his voice. "Not that it couldn't be arranged," he says, "if I wanted, but it's . . . not the case."

"You don't like to arrange it, huh?"

"No, I'd prefer it in the nature of a surprise," Mr. Carlisle says. "That's what I'd like."

DOING THE KROPOTKA

"What's the word for window in Russian?" Stanley says, pointing to the window. It is the end of the meal. Dessert is being served.

Beryl frowns. "Oh dear, I can't remember . . . What *is* it now?"

"You don't know the word for window?" Stanley laughs. "What is this? Here your husband was telling me last night you're the world's biggest expert on Russian literature and you don't even know *window*?"

Beryl flushes to the tips of her ears. "I can't remember it," she says desperately. "Is it ok——"

"Kropotka!" Stanley says triumphantly. "That's what it is! Kropotka! How does that sound to you?"

"Kropotka?" Beryl looks puzzled. "No, it doesn't ring a bell. I don't know, maybe."

"You don't know *kropotka*?" Stanley says, staring at her.

Beryl swallows. "Well, it's just, it doesn't sound like the word I remember."

"What's pencil?" Stanley says.

"Pencil? *Karandash,*" Beryl says, relieved she remembers something at least.

"What's spoon?" he says, waving the spoon at her.

"Spoon? Oh help, I always forget these things. Spoon . . ."

Stanley shakes his head. "What is this? She's studying Russian and she doesn't know any of the common nouns. What *does* she know?"

"We mainly learned to read," Beryl says quietly. "Turgenev and—"

"Not just to read," says Patrick who is getting slightly high, "but to understand—to understand what was not understood before."

While Patrick is coming upstairs, Beryl gets out her Russian dictionary and looks up window. It is *okno.* She smiles with satisfaction.

"Window is *okno,*" she says to Patrick as he enters the room. "I was right."

"So you should have been more forceful," Patrick says.

She draws away angrily, remembering him and Linda at dinner. "The old fool!" she says. "Kropotka! Where'd he get that, for God's sake? What does kropotka mean? It doesn't mean *anything.*"

Patrick raises his eyebrows. "You know what 'doing the kropotka' means in Russian dialect," he says dryly.

Beryl can't help smiling. "That's true," she says, joining in with his tone. "I'd forgotten about that."

"Naturally the term isn't used much in polite society," Patrick says.

"I should hope not," Beryl says.

Patrick lies down on the bed, pulling her down also. He smiles. "How about doing the kropotka?" he says. "What do you say?"

A MOZART DIVERTIMENTO OR
THAT DISGUSTING MAN

As soon as they settle down at the concert, Beryl begins thinking of Stanley and how terrible he is. She scarcely hears the music and cannot even sink back and enjoy the pleasant fantasies that Mozart usually stirs up in her. Instead, she sits tensely, staring ahead with a frown. Between the movements of the divertimento, Patrick leans over and whispers with a smile, "That was nice, wasn't it?"

Beryl turns on him a stony glance. "I haven't been listening," she says.

"Why?" He looks disturbed. "What's wrong?"

"I just feel horribly depressed," Beryl says, tearing a small piece off the corner of the program.

"Why though, honey?"

"*You* know why." Her mouth turns down with an aggrieved expression. "Because of *him*," she says. "He was so awful."

The music starts again, the strings beginning a light allegro.

"It's not worth making such a fuss over," Patrick whispers. "Just sit back and enjoy the music."

"I can't," Beryl hisses.

"Hey! Quiet there!" someone in front of her calls, and a dignified lady in a broad-rimmed straw hat turns around and frowns at them disapprovingly.

"We'll discuss it later," Patrick whispers.

"I'm going to ask to be transferred to another table," Beryl says as they stand on the lawn during intermission. "I won't sit with him for one more meal."

"Well . . ." Patrick looks as though he cannot decide which will have a worse result—crossing his wife or causing a disturbance by changing the seating arrangement.

"I want you to speak to Signora Montini tonight," Beryl

says. "As soon as we get back." She does not look at him as she speaks but looks at a family that is sitting under a tree, gaily drinking wine and eating sandwiches, although it has started to rain. They look so happy!

"All right, I'll speak to her," Patrick says, "if you're sure you want—"

"Yes," Beryl says. "I will not sit with that disgusting man one more day!"

Mr. Carlisle, standing unseen in back of them, stiffens. It does not for one instant occur to him that the "disgusting man" Beryl referred to could be anyone but himself. He is as startled as if, entering a post office, he saw his own face looming down from a Wanted list.

He will leave the next day! He had only planned to stay a day or so longer anyway. Leave quietly before breakfast, pay up his bill, and be gone. Avoid unpleasantness. In a way he would like to apologize to all of them. But for what? He is as vague about what exactly his crime has been as he is that, whatever it is, he has been guilty of it. He leaves before the concert is over, leaves right in the middle of a Mozart wind quintet that he especially likes, and hurries home to pack. He will pack before Jimmy returns and will pretend to be asleep.

So he does—lying stiffly in bed, heart beating thunderously, gazing through half-shut eyes as the boy, unconscious of being watched, strips, walks naked to the window, gazes out a moment at some insect pinioned to the screen. The poignancy of his innocent, relaxed body, like some bar from the half-heard Mozart, makes Mr. Carlisle want to weep.

The next morning, by breakfast, he is on the road to Paris.

SEPARATE TABLES

The next morning—they are to leave the following afternoon—Beryl and Patrick are seated at a table for two in a far corner of the dining room. They sit in stiff silence, Patrick abstracted, Beryl staring rigidly out at the view.

When Linda comes in, she doesn't see them at first and simply sits down at their usual table. Guilia comes around to take the orders for the main course. At that moment, looking up, Linda catches Patrick's eye and walks over to their table.

"Hi! How'd you two get squashed over here?" she says cheerfully.

There is a moment of silence.

Then Beryl, looking down at her plate, says, "It's because of your husband."

"Stanley? What—he had you put here? Oh God, some joke or something?"

"No, it's—" This time Beryl raises her head and looks directly at Linda. "We don't want to sit with him." When Linda says nothing, she rushes on, "He's a horrible person—a cruel, vindictive, mean person, I never want to speak to him again."

Linda flushes, then smiles. "Or to me?"

"It's not you," Beryl says. "It's him."

"Am I to sit with him alone, then?"

"He's your husband," Beryl says desperately. She looks at Patrick, but he is watching the two of them with what seems to be total detachment—it is to be her battle, not his. "Why did you marry him? Why don't you divorce him?"

At that moment Stanley, coming into the dining room, sees the three of them—Linda is still standing, her hands resting on her white straw pocketbook—and walks briskly over. "So? Where's the chow?" he says. "What's up?"

"She wants to know why I don't divorce you," Linda says, pointing to Beryl.

Stanley reddens, then laughs. "She does, eh? Good question."

"She thinks you're a cruel, vindictive, mean person—am I quoting right?" She smiles at Beryl.

Beryl, aghast, watches her. What side was Linda on?

"Well, you're not such a little sweetie yourself," Stanley says.

"Cut it out, Stanley," Linda says.

"Huh? *I* should cut it out? I walk in the dining room and right away I'm a mean, vindictive son of a bitch."

"Not right away," Beryl says. "Always."

Linda says, "We should sit down and eat. Guilia's motioning to us." She walks away silently.

Stanley, arms akimbo, looks at Patrick. "I'd hate to tell you what I think of your wife, 'cause it might not be polite at the dinner table . . . But it's your piece of pie. You eat it."

Alone, Beryl looks at Patrick. He is watching her with a grave, severe expression. "Why did you let him say those things?" she says, her lip quivering.

He says nothing.

"He destroys everything!" she says wildly. "Everything!" In tears she flees the dining room.

Patrick finishes his meal by himself.

THE BENEFITS OF REST

"Well, Louis hied himself off, evidently," Stanley says. "Signora Montini says he left before breakfast."

Linda, folding one of her dresses, says, without looking up, "I'm sorry."

"What a weirdo." Stanley rolls a tie up in a ball. "I mean it . . . Still, you were right. He wasn't interested in Jimmy much . . . that I could see."

"No," Linda says.

"No, what?"

"No, he wasn't interested in . . . Jimmy."

"You can't figure those types," Stanley says. "They're a

bag of neuroses. They don't know what they want themselves."

"I wonder why he left so soon," Linda says. Darkly tanned, she looks like an underexposed negative, her hair white, her face burnished.

"Soon? It wasn't so soon."

"Without saying good-bye."

"Oh well . . . Had to get moving, I guess."

"I guess." She is finished packing. She stands and watches thoughtfully, as Stanley tucks the last shirt in the valise. He looks up and grins.

"You look great, kid. Really. The rest did you some good."

For once Linda smiles. "Yes, maybe it did."

AS FAR AS SEX GOES

Patrick is loading their luggage. Beryl stands in the shade, watching him. She is pregnant. She has suspected it for several days now, and watching Patrick, a great pang of hunger assails her, though she has eaten breakfast just an hour before. Nearby Linda is saying something to Signora Montini. Beryl is aware of her in a bright blue dress moving off to one side.

Linda comes up beside Beryl. "He *is* a son of a bitch," she says. "You're right."

Beryl says, "No, I didn't mean—"

"Sure you did . . . Only, that's the way it is. That's life."

"Is it?"

"Who knows?"

"Why don't you . . . have lovers?" Beryl asks timidly.

"They're not so easy to come by."

"Why?"

"Well, some are married, some are—"

"Patrick would have slept with you," Beryl says bravely.

Linda smiles. "Well . . ."

"He would've. You should have. I'm nothing special as far as sex goes." This self-abasement comes from the overwhelming feeling that she had upon first seeing her, that Linda is the most beautiful person she has ever met.

Linda is silent. Five years later—when she is divorced from Stanley who marries a red-haired heiress from Oklahoma City, interested in the opera; when she is living alone in a five-room Park Avenue apartment with a color TV, a thrice-divorced boyfriend, age fifty-five, who has suffered one heart attack and may suffer another, and two Afghan hounds—Linda remembers this conversation with Beryl. How she remembers it, what it means to her, is ambiguous. That there was another kind of life she might have led, that she had been capable, occasionally, of kindness as well as bitchiness (she did not seduce Patrick), that—but there are many variations, depending on her mood. At the moment, standing beside Beryl, she just says lightly, casually, "I hope you'll be very happy."

Beryl bites her lips. She is dizzy. "Yes, I hope so . . . We want to have a large family," she says suddenly, wanting to mention her secret to Linda, but hesitant.

"Yes, children are a great—they can be a—"

Stanley, who has just paid the bill, comes over and pats Beryl's bare brown belly. "Got a little bundle in there?" he says, smiling broadly.

How did *he* know? How did *he* guess? Beryl feels indignant.

"Kiddies are a great hobby," he says, winking. To Patrick, who has just appeared, he says, "Keep up the good work, buddy."

Turning, Beryl vomits into the nearby bushes.

INTO THE SUNSET

"Are you trying to kill us?"

Beryl, bouncing forward, konks her head against the front window as Patrick swerves to avoid a motorcycle.

Patrick turns to face her but says nothing. For a long moment their eyes confront each other. Then he reaches out and touches her hand. "I'm sorry, darling."

Beryl's lip trembles. She looks straight ahead, trying to decide how soon it should be before she will forgive him.

Jimmy, from the backseat of the Tomlinsons' car, sees them and waves, but they do not notice. He returns to eating grapes.

HAPPINESS IS . . .

They are not chasing him. After driving an hour, Mr. Carlisle gradually loosens his grip on the wheel—his hands are red from pressing—and leans back in the seat. His back is stiff. He arches it. He has escaped. He is free. And, after all, it is a nice day out. He looks around, sighs. The sun is shining; the trees hang over the road; the air, still morning, is fresh. Why rush? Why be anxious? He will get where he is going soon enough. There's no hurry.

EASTER RABBITS IN JULY

Because their spouses were presumably in love, or at any rate having an affair, Irving Shapiro and Miriam Kandinsky decided to sleep together, too. They had known each other ten years and neither was in the least in love with the other. They scarcely liked each other, in fact. But it seemed, meeting outside the lawyer's office one scorching July afternoon, a fitting thing to do, an expression of mutual discontent. However, Irving's apartment, to which they repaired after a few drinks at a local cocktail lounge, was not air-conditioned and the mood of elation and devil-may-care rapidly disintegrated into sweaty irritation. Miriam, for her part, was furious.

"What an idiotic idea," she said, sitting up in bed. "What in hell is wrong with us to have thought of a thing like this?" She looked angrily at Irving, demanding an answer. She was a stout, handsome girl with dark hair drawn back in a school-teacher's bun and harlequin eyeglasses.

Irving, small, fragile, totally bald at thirty, had the sheet draped around him like a Bedouin. "You're right, I suppose," he said.

"Revenge!" Miriam said. "Will you tell me how *this* revenges anyone? Even if they knew they wouldn't care!

They'd hoot with laughter. They'd laugh themselves *sick!"*

Such violence disturbed Irving, who was feeling a little queasy anyway. He remembered Miriam arguing about politics at dinner parties and how he had always regarded her as a somewhat frightening, not very subtle participant. "I don't regret it, anyway," he said.

This reply seemed to exasperate Miriam still further, "What was the point in it?" she wanted to know. "Will you tell me that?"

"So, maybe there was no point," Irving acknowledged. "So? There's no point in most things."

Such defeatism seemed to Miriam the last straw. How could Gina ever have married him? How could anyone have? He couldn't even mix a dry martini. She remembered asking for one once at their house. Irving had said, "I'm not really sure . . . No one's ever asked me for a martini before."

Miriam stood up and began to dress. She took a morose pleasure in the fact that being seen naked by Irving was a neutral occasion—like Egyptian princesses being seen by their slaves, she thought.

"You know, you don't dress well," Irving said, watching her.

Miriam was fastening the buttons of her dress. "What do you mean?" She took her brush out of her purse and began fixing her hair, twisting it up into its familiar bun.

"Like that dress," Irving said.

"What's wrong with it?"

"It's an ugly color, that shade of green. I don't like it."

"Well, screw you . . . I do."

"You don't have a sense of style," he said, but thoughtfully, quietly, as though considering an abstract point. "Some women do, some don't."

Disgusted, secretly hurt, Miriam turned her back to him and began fixing her hair.

"You're a reasonably attractive woman," Irving said, "but

who would know it? With your hair gnarled up like that?
Like some old babushka." He stood up and, unexpectedly,
took the brush out of Miriam's hand. The sheet remained
draped loosely around him.

He looks like Gandhi, Miriam thought. She stood obediently while he fiddled with her hair, pulling out bobby
pins, brushing it loose over her shoulders. Finally he stood
back a little to admire the effect, like a painter before a
canvas. "That's not exactly what I had in mind," he said,
"but you get the idea."

Impassively Miriam regarded her image in the full-length
mirror. "It's too hot to wear it loose," she said. "Anyway, I'm
too old for this style."

"How old *are* you?"

"Thirty-six."

"*That's* not old."

"It's old." She piled the hair up again as it had been, getting down on her hands and knees to search for the bobby
pins. Irving, seated on the bed, admired with sad detachment
her buttocks as she stooped and searched. "You have good
qualities, Miriam," he assured her. "Your age doesn't
matter."

"Irving, will you do me a favor?" Miriam said. "Just shut
up."

"That's what I mean," said Irving, unperturbed. "It's your
manner. You have to learn to be more yielding and feminine
at moments like this."

"Moments like what?" Miriam wanted to know. She
sighed heavily. "Why don't you have an air conditioner at
least?"

"I did," he said. "Gina took it."

"So, you couldn't get another one? . . . Look at this apartment, too." Dressed now but barefoot, she wandered into the
living room. "It's a mess. Dust all over everything." She ges-
tured wildly. "Don't you have a cleaning lady?"

"I did," Irving said mournfully. "Gina took *her* too."

"This apartment is filthy," Miriam said. "How can you live here?"

"It is dirty, I guess," Irving said. He stood in the doorway, arms folded across his chest, watching restless, angry Miriam. He cleared his throat. "Are you hungry, Miriam? Would you like something to eat?"

"I'd like a dry martini," Miriam said and then guffawed loudly.

Irving looked at her in bewilderment; he didn't know what was funny.

An hour later they emerged from the apartment and began walking along Eighth Street. Miriam said, "Isn't it dangerous with all these hippies around?"

"I don't know," Irving said. "I never thought about it . . . No one's ever tried to rape me," he added, smiling slyly.

"*That's* not surprising."

"Neighborhoods—they're all the same. Those things don't affect me."

They walked in silence past bookstores, pastry shops, boutiques with elegant and colorful clothing. Before one window Irving stood transfixed at a large display of multicolored stuffed animals. "I *should* get her a present," he said.

"Who?"

"Paula . . . She'll be five next week."

"Let's go in, then." Paula was one of his daughters—skinny, nasty little kids, Miriam thought. They peed on the living room floor for free expression, and once when Miriam was visiting, the younger one kept saying, "Why is your nose so long?"

They entered the store.

It might have been inconsiderate, Irving thought, to have brought Miriam into a children's toy store. When she was barren. But was she? Gina had said so. They must have discussed it. But wasn't there something about how Dick, as a rabbi, wouldn't allow a semen sample to be taken? So they would never know. Presumably a barren rabbi would be a bad thing, no matter what congregation you belonged to . . . But it was sad, anyway, poor barren Miriam. He had been thoughtless. And he thought, secretly, with pleasure of his little girls whose soft flowerlike vaginas he had delicately washed so many times and who leaned against him with heavy, sweet drowsiness coming home from the Children's Zoo.

Irving collected electric trains. Miriam remembered this now, watching him browse down the aisle, peering at various elaborate setups. It was typical—his retarded ways. Living in a child's world. Living? He was dead. And *she* was crazy. I am a crazy person, Miriam told herself, to have undergone intercourse or any form of sexual contact for that matter with someone like Irving Shapiro. There is no excuse for that. I will not get ahead that way.

On one table there was a large heap of Easter rabbits in varying pastel shades—yellow, blue, pink. SALE! a sign announced dramatically. DRASTIC REDUCTIONS.

Irving approached the table. "Those are nice," he said. "But why are they on sale? Are they defective?"

Miriam shrugged. "I guess there's not much demand for Easter rabbits in July."

Behind them a saleslady materialized from nowhere, smiling unctuously. "They have *small* defects," she said. "Very minor."

Irving held one rabbit by the ears and turned it around slowly. It was a yellow rabbit with blue whiskers. "Do you see anything wrong with this one?" he asked Miriam.

"One eye is missing," Miriam said flatly.

He set it down and rummaged among the others. Finally, he held up another, a smaller, pink one. "How's this for size, bubbela?"

His jocularity oppressed her. What would the saleslady think they were? Lovers, God forbid? He's my uncle, she wanted to say. He's my lawyer, he's my great-aunt. "It looks okay," she said.

Irving turned the rabbit upside down; he shook it; nothing happened. "I like this rabbit," he said. "It has more character than that other one . . . Don't you think?"

"Definitely," Miriam said.

"I'm going to buy this rabbit," Irving said. He was pleased. He brought the rabbit to the saleslady. "Ordinarily I'm indecisive when it comes to children's toys," he said to Miriam, "but this rabbit appealed to me somehow . . . Something about it."

"It has nice whiskers," Miriam said.

Irving looked at her suspiciously. "It doesn't have whiskers."

They stood together and watched as the saleslady placed the rabbit in a white box, wrapped it in tissue paper, closed the box, wrapped the box in striped paper and tied it with a large bow.

But five minutes later, as they were turning down Bleecker, Irving said morosely, "There's probably something wrong with that rabbit we didn't notice . . . I should have gotten a fresh one."

"It's okay. Don't worry about it," Miriam said.

"It *looked* all right," conceded Irving dubiously, "but you never can tell."

"Want to drop it off now?" Miriam suggested. They were near the hotel in which Gina had rented a two-room suite with the girls. The suite with Irving's air conditioner and Irving's cleaning lady and her husband.

"Should I?" Irving said.

"You could . . . It's nearby."

"What if we run into them?"

"So? Big deal."

"You're right. *They're* the ones that should worry."

He had morbid, perverse thoughts of coming in on them having intercourse. Even before the separation he had brooded on irrelevancies: angles, positions, degree of undress, possible fetishes. Did it prove he was a fag? Unconscious desires for a rabbi? But I don't believe in God! A pervert then? More simply, a voyeur? Gina's pubic hair was very pale, red almost, a curious fact that stirred Irving's memory like the thought of some birthmark in a private place. Red like some kind of forest moss.

They saw Gina even before they reached the hotel. She was on the other side of the street, walking in the opposite direction from them. She was wearing white slacks and a bright blue blouse. A long blond ponytail swung jauntily in back of her. She walked slowly, saunteringly, with feet out, like the ex-modern dancer she was. Seeing her, Irving turned green.

"Let's turn here," Miriam said. She didn't want him fainting in the middle of Sullivan Street. What did you do with a fainting anthropologist? She who didn't know beans about artificial respiration.

"I refuse to run away," he said, balking. "That's ignominious."

"It's not running away," Miriam said. "It's just—"

"I'm going to go over right now and give her this present," Irving said. He straightened up.

"You *are?*" Miriam looked at him anxiously.

"Yes."

"Well, should I wait here for you or what?"

But he was off, unhearing. Oh Irving, you child, you idiot. Had he aroused Gina's maternal instinct? He'll be hit by a car, Miriam thought. God, I can't watch. She half expected Gina to rise up, dragonlike, and devour Irving. She would have to gather the bones in her bag and carry them off.

Irving handed Gina the present. Gina took it.

He scarcely heard her words. It was like a pantomime play, like the TV with the sound turned off. He saw Gina's eyes, which were angry, her pink, perspiring face, the baby, sleeping belly down (and whose was it, anyway?). He spoke, she spoke, and in a moment the present was stuffed in the carriage and she had wheeled off, her buttocks moving angrily in the white slacks. And someone, an elderly man in a plaid coat, was watching them lecherously. And he, Irving, was standing, alone, on a streetcorner. He was mad. For he still loved her in the most abject, childlike way and would, had it been possible, have converted himself to some small baby-shape to be held to her breast, comforted by her, allowed to squeal with rage at frustrated desire.

The last time all four of them had been together, Miriam thought, waiting, was in a discothèque not far from here. They had met "by chance" outside a movie, a revival of some W. C. Fields thing. In the smoky dark Gina had whirled and danced. She and Irving had watched. Irving drank a great deal of Scotch and soda and began describing an article he was writing about the eating habits of some Eskimo group. Miriam had thought: Irving has his Eskimos and I have nothing. She wished she had had children. She wished she had a skill, an asset, could walk a tightrope or sing leide or make napoleons. I want a skill, Miriam thought as her husband had whirled with her former college roommate, feeling her up in the smoky room.

Irving reappeared. He looked more green.

"Irving, you are ill," Miriam told him.

"I would like something to eat," Irving said, speaking very slowly and distinctly, like a child learning to read. "I feel very hungry."

"Did she like the present?"

"She didn't open it."

"How did she act?"

"I don't want to talk about it."

"All right."

They went into a small coffeehouse where chamber music was playing in the background. The waiter in tight dark pants and a print shirt handed them large, elaborately inscribed menus. "I'll have a cheeseburger and expresso," Miriam said.

The waiter looked inquiringly at Irving. "I'll have a—" he began and then stopped. The waiter and Miriam looked at him, alarmed and curious. "I'll have a—" he said. His mouth remained open as though he were going to continue speaking; then suddenly he put his head in his hands and began to weep.

"We'll have two expressos," Miriam said hastily. For several moments she sat, detached, scornful, sad, looking at Irving. She lit a cigarette. "Don't," she said finally. "It's not worth it."

"She doesn't love me anymore," he mumbled into a handkerchief he had fished out of somewhere.

"Well, that's the way it is," Miriam said. "That's life."

He looked up. "Paula doesn't even like rabbits . . . She *hates* them, in fact. A rabbit bit her once at school. Why did I get her a rabbit?"

"You forgot."

"I could have gotten a doll. What's *wrong* with me?"

"You're fine, Irving," Miriam said. "There's nothing wrong with you."

When it came, Irving ate Miriam's cheeseburger. He ate two eclairs, one chocolate, one mocha. At the end, blowing his nose loudly, he said, "You're a kind person, Miriam."

"No, I'm not," Miriam said.

"You're the kindest person I've ever met," Irving said. "I wish I was in love with you."

He asked if she would spend the weekend with him. To her surprise, she found herself saying she would. On an uprise of hope, disappointment, the sweetness of the eclairs, the sadness of the chamber music, they left the coffeehouse.

And they did, in fact, spend the entire weekend together. On Friday Miriam cleaned Irving's apartment. On Friday night they saw an off-Broadway play and watched the late, late show. On Saturday Irving bought an air conditioner. On Saturday night they got drunk on crème de menthe, the only liquor Gina had left behind. On Sunday they both felt sick. Irving lay in bed with a hot water bottle. Miriam took cold showers, drank tomato juice, and read the last half of *Gone with the Wind* (which Gina had also left behind). Then on Monday they parted and did not see each other again for five years. They met at a party. Both slightly high, they laughed and joked and their mutual spouses (new ones) cast suspicious glances, seeing, in this easy jocularity, proof of a tender and long-lived affair that, quite naturally, had never been mentioned.

SOMEONE'S FACE AT THE DOOR

"How did she do it?" Gisela asked. They were sitting at the counter of Schrafft's having lunch.

"I don't know," Edward said. "They didn't say. Pills, I imagine."

"Why that?"

"It would have been easiest since her father's a doctor. There was always a lot of medication around the house."

"Didn't he realize and hide them?"

"How could he?" He set down his coffee. "She just would've found some other way."

She covered his hand with hers. "Has it upset you a great deal?"

He smiled wryly. "A great deal? No, I don't know. In a way not, actually."

"Because you knew it would happen eventually?"

"Not knew," he said. "One can't know these things for certain . . . I suspected, I'd thought of it . . . But the main thing is, she was a stranger to me by now."

"But you saw her every week when you went to pick up Richard?"

"Yes, saw her—but what does that tell you? Someone's face

at the door, a fleeting impression, a word or two. And I suppose I tried not to find out, not to ask."

"You had your own life?"

"And she hers, as far as I knew."

"Do you feel guilty about it?"

He hesitated. "No," he said. "I don't see why I should. If there was something I genuinely felt I could have done, it would be different. But I said all those things—a million times—when I was married to her. After a certain point—" He waved his hand in the air, "there's a feeling of futility . . . Do you want dessert?"

"Maybe some coffee . . . Do you mind?"

"Not at all. We're early, anyway."

She reached for the sugar. "Will they mind, your bringing me?" she said.

"I don't care if they do."

"You should."

"Why?"

"If you want Richard. Won't they be able to keep him?"

"How? I'm his legal father. I don't see how they could possibly unless I'd signed the rights away."

For a moment she was silent. "Do you want him?" she said.

His face changed; it looked older, more tired. "I think I do," he said. "Yes, I think so." He began stirring his coffee around and around. "It's such a change," he said. "This is the thing that will be hard to get used to. I feel now I work all day—all my energies have gone there, almost all. And now, here he is, seven years old. Sure, I've seen him every week, but an hour a week, two hours, three—think of the difference between that and every day living. It's like the difference between a Saturday night date and marriage."

She smiled.

He continued looking at her, studying her, although he knew his intent scrutiny made her nervous. Her hand was curved around the coffee cup and that hand, round, tanned, with short-cut nails had for him an impression of health and security that pleased him. It was not just that she looked unlike Sylvia, not a matter of features. It was little things, the fact that she ate heartily and with good appetite, instead of just picking at her food; that she had an open, even noisy laugh that seemed to spill out, rather than a tense spasm of giggles; that when she walked it was with a flat-footed, almost ungraceful stride, not a slow, mincing, almost sliding movement. In the past, when he had been married to Sylvia, he had had a Botticelli maiden as an ideal—long flowing hair, vague, dreamy eyes, emaciated, drifting body. Now, when he passed these in the museum—he was a curator at the Metropolitan—he hurried past, almost afraid to look at them, as though those eyes would catch him and fix him with their relentless sadness. He found himself visiting, for pleasure, the rooms with the Dutch and Flemish women, the laughing Hals barmaid with her hands on her hips and her hair tousled.

When they emerged, the sun was out, but it was still very cold. He took her hand and put it in his pocket, warming it in his. "You should wear gloves," he said.

"I should."

They crossed the street.

"What an elegant building," she said. "Pretty posh."

"He's a psychiatrist."

She raised her eyebrows.

They entered the lobby of the building. The doorman darted forward. "Who are you going to see, sir?" he said.

"Klingman. Thomas Klingman," he said.

"Very good, sir. Who shall I say is arriving?"

"They expect us," he said curtly. These formalities always irritated him. He walked past, leaving the doorman standing there with his mouth open.

The lobby was about fifty feet long, lined on one side

completely with gray marble. The other side opened out into
a formal garden with clipped hedges. It had always reminded
him of the set of a movie; somehow it always seemed to be
deserted, although the building itself must have housed
thousands of tenants. There was an elevator man in the elevator, even though it was automatic. This, too, annoyed him,
to think of this man being hired, in his white gloves and blue
uniform, just to press a row of little buttons.

As they got out of the elevator, Gisela said, "My God,
what are they going to do with a place like this when the
revolution comes?"

Edward smiled dryly. "I don't think they're too worried
about that."

The lobby, carpeted from one end to the other, stretched
endlessly, with doors on either side.

"If I lived here," Gisela said, "I think I'd have a tremendous temptation to run screaming down this hall in the
nude."

"What it's always reminded me of," Edward said, "is those
scenes in the madhouse painted by Van Gogh—you know,
the sense of constriction."

His inlaws had a large mat outside their door, with *Klingman* printed in large red letters. With one finger Edward
lightly touched the bell. It gave off a series of elaborate
chimes. A moment later the seeing-eye lifted up. His former
mother-in-law was very nervous, and despite the fact that the
building was loaded with doormen, she was as cautious in
admitting people as though she were living in a tenement on
the Lower East Side. She was quite the opposite of his former father-in-law, who spoke joshingly of renting the apartment across the street in which a violent and still unsolved
murder had taken place a few months ago. "Think how low
the rent will be," he said. "No one will want to move in. It's
a perfect opportunity."

"Edward, hello," said Mrs. Klingman. Her glance darted to

Gisela, who smiled politely. She looked a little suspicious, as though he had brought with him a dripping wet sheep dog who would climb all over the furniture.

"This is Gisela Eisner," he said.

Mrs. Klingman smiled tightly. "Delighted to meet you," she said. She continued for a moment to stand at the door, not letting them enter the apartment. For a moment he had a vision of customs, of her checking through his pockets to see if he was carrying any loaded arms. She was a small woman, not much over five feet, well preserved. Her hair, although she was in her sixties, displayed not a trace of gray; she fluffed it into some red-brown poodlelike effect. Dressed neatly, trimly, she had always seemed to him to look older, through her dieting, than his own mother, who was twice as stout and had had white hair since she was forty-five. Like her husband, she wore "space shoes," which looked strange compared to the rest of her resolutely chic figure, like heavy webbed feet. He saw Gisela glance at the shoes and could not help the faintest of smiles.

"Where is the doctor?" he said, as they walked into the front hall and his mother-in-law closed the door behind him. He found himself, as he had in the past, adopting a formal, slightly sarcastic tone in this house, which he knew did not endear him to her.

"Here I am, Edward," his former father-in-law called from the living room.

Edward, looking into the spacious and elaborately decorated room, saw Dr. Klingman seated near the window in a brocade chair. Across his knees was a gaily colored cloth that, as Edward approached, turned out to be a rug with a pattern of red, yellow, white and black, suggesting the motif of some Southwestern tribe. "Hello, hello," the elderly man greeted them jovially. "How do you like this?"

"What is it?" Gisela asked politely. Edward could see by her tone she was fascinated.

"Why, it's a rug, my dear, a rug."

"You're making a rug?"

"Yes, so I am. It's my second, in fact. I've made another. Would you like it? I haven't the vaguest idea what to do with it when I'm finished."

"Then why are you making it?" she asked.

"Therapy, therapy, my dear. My own diagnosis. They say doctors shouldn't diagnose themselves. Nonsense! Who else knows what's good for them as well as they do? Yes, there's nothing like it. It's as good as a bottle of Valium. After I retired, I got restless just sitting around. Oh, I still work part of the day, but this is the very thing . . . What do you think of the colors? Too bright? What do you say, Edward? You're the connoisseur."

"Edward wouldn't like a rug," his wife interjected quickly. The three of them were standing in a semicircle around the older man. "It's not *that* kind of art he's interested in."

"I think it's interesting," Edward said. "Maybe I should take it up myself."

"No doubt about it. You should, by all means." Sitting there, round and rosy, with scarcely a thread of hair left on his head, the elderly man made a quaint and comic sight with the Indian rug on his lap. Edward felt certain he knew the doctor was devoted to eccentricities and courted them, as though they were beautiful women, perhaps because in his professional life he had always had to be so scrupulously colorless. Edward continued looking at him. The lack of reference to Sylvia or her death was typical of the doctor and did not surprise him. He was a man of such total reserve about personal matters that Edward had always suspected his deeper feelings were revealed only when he was alone, like etchings so delicate they would rot from contact with the common air. Whether this was to counteract the emotionality, even hysteria, of his wife or just a by now well-worn tendency, he had never been certain. Dr. Klingman might,

for all he or, he suspected, anyone would ever know, be broken by his daughter's death, shattered; yet, like someone with
a malignant cancer who continued to walk and talk normally,
he would hide this fact under a thousand idle jests and quips.

"Where is Richard now?" he said, turning to Mrs. Klingman, who continued to regard her husband with faint annoyance; evidently the rug-making did not meet with her
approval.

"He's down in the park with Alma," Mrs. Klingman said,
her disapproval seeming to shift subtly to Edward.

He was silent a moment. "I see . . . Will he be back soon?"

"Yes, he should be back for lunch," Mrs. Klingman said.

Her tone suggested several things. One, the emphasis on
Alma. This meant, You see, we are quite able to take care of
the child ourselves. We have a full-time maid who takes him
to the park. You could scarcely afford such a luxury. By
changing this routine, you will only interfere. Also, she
seemed to make no reference to the fact that he had come
for a definite purpose. It was he who might have been the
visitor, the intruder, the unfamiliar uncle come to spend the
afternoon. But because these suspicions were all underground so far, he could not meet them by any open word or
action.

". . . in art history too?" Mrs. Klingman was saying to
Gisela.

"No, I work on Wall Street," Gisela replied.

"Wall Street! Just the woman I need," said Dr. Klingman.
"Do you know anything about stocks?"

"A bit."

"My dear, we must have a talk. You don't happen to have
heard of a coming merger between Allied Chemical and Gulf
Sulfur?"

"No, I'm not sure," Gisela said. "I don't think I did."

Edward, watching her, judging without wanting to judge,
felt that she would make a good impression on the doctor.

He was a man who appreciated women, not a ladies' man necessarily. She had dressed decently—Edward was glad of that, particularly since, as a rule, she was careless and indifferent about clothes. But her dark suit and high heels gave the impression of a certain European formality and dignity—all to the good. And her manner—hesitant, polite, reserved—this was a good thing as well. But then he felt angry. Why feel on stage? What if they didn't like her? What business was it of theirs? Who cared what they thought! Feeling tense, Edward walked across the room and looked out the window. Below, far below, was the park. They were much too high up to be able to detect any figures, but he fancied that in certain amorphous shapes he might be seeing Richard, playing there.

Gisela walked over next to him. "What a beautiful view," she said.

"Yes," murmured Edward, still angry but trying not to show it.

"Let me show you the rest of the house," Dr. Klingman said, "as long as we have to wait."

"That would be lovely," said Gisela.

He was left alone with his former mother-in-law.

"What a nice young woman," she said in a voice that chilled him slightly.

He tried to smile. "I think so," he said.

"Is she German? Her accent—"

"She escaped from East Germany about six years ago."

"Oh. I see."

There was a light pause. He looked at her puzzled—what? Oh, of course! Why hadn't he thought of that? German. Jewish. Bringing a goy into the house. And yet somehow he never thought of the Klingmans as being that religious. He doubted they were. But prejudices were strong enough, anyway. A wry bitter smile appeared on his face. "Yes, she's

German," he repeated, for no reason other than to meet his
mother-in-law's eye and to be able to express, by his intonation, I know your lousy suspicions and I don't give a damn
for them.

"You're thinking of marriage?" Mrs. Klingman said in that
cold, trying-to-be interested voice.

"We—I—we're not certain yet," Edward said. "It's certainly a possibility." He paused a moment. "But, you see,
Gisela was married once also and so she, too, has certain . . .
hesitations."

His mother-in-law's expression seemed an effort to reduce
him to nothingness. "Hesitations?" she repeated. "You mean
about your ability to be a good mate?"

The word *mate* struck Edward as peculiar. "That," he said
carefully, "but also a desire to find the right person."

"You know, Edward," she said. "Marriage is not a matter
of finding the right person, but of *being* the right person."

This little cliché, so like her, riled him. The sense of rage
that had been stirring in him since he set foot in the apartment started to rise. He turned away from her, not trusting
himself to speak.

"Marriage is responsibilities," she went on in the same unc-
tuous voice, "duties, sacrifices, not just flitting from one pleasure to another. It—"

He whirled around. "How dare you talk to me like this?"
he said. "Do you think I don't know these things? Is this your
conception of why Sylvia and I failed? Have you blocked out
the truth to that extent that not even her death will make
you realize—"

She was weeping. He felt a sudden dead feeling, a mixture
of pity and regret. Why had he been so harsh? But all this
vanished in an instant when she said, "You—you killed her. It
was your fault, your fault."

He felt close to weeping himself, with sheer despair and

incomprehension. "It's my fault she was unhappy?" he said. "My fault? You know she was always like that. You know that was why our marriage went to pieces."

"If you had stayed by, tried to help her—"

"I didn't try? I didn't try with every goddamn muscle in my body for six years?" Edward said. "How can you say a thing like that? My God! Who tried if I didn't? You? Your husband?"

"We gave her everything," Mrs. Klingman said. "Tell me what we spared. How is it our fault?"

"It wasn't your fault," Edward said. "This is the point. It wasn't your fault any more than it was mine."

"Then whose fault was it?" she demanded.

"No one's," he said. "Why must it be a matter of fault?"

They stood in silence, looking at each other. Edward took out a cigarette, lit it, and walked over to the piano. He had given up smoking a month ago, but at the moment his desire for a cigarette was too strong to resist. "Will you keep the piano?" he said after a moment. It had been Sylvia who played the piano. Often, in the evening, when he was in his study working, he would hear the sounds of some Beethoven sonata, muted, soft.

"I don't know," his mother-in-law said in a much softer voice. "I—we haven't decided yet."

Edward glanced at his watch; it was nearly two o'clock. "Won't Richard be getting hungry?" he said. "It's a little late for lunch."

For a moment she did not reply.

"It's after two," he said, looking at her curiously. "Did he have a late breakfast?"

"He's not coming up," she said.

He stared at her. "What do you mean?"

"I told Alma to keep him out all afternoon."

"But you knew I was coming. What was the point in it?"

"You'll take him away," she said. "That's what you came

for. Well, I won't let you. He belongs to us. He's all we have
left. You can't take him, too."

"That's absurd," he said. "You mean, I won't be allowed
to see my own son—"

"You have your own life, your job, your interests, your
girls," she said, almost spitting out the last word. "What do
you need him for?"

Without a word, Edward walked through to the next
room. Dr. Klingman was pointing to a painting on the wall, a
vivid splash of red on white.

"Is it a bird?" Gisela was saying. "Somehow the movement
suggests to me—"

"Well, I think the painter had in mind something less
literal," Dr. Klingman said, "a—"

Edward seized Gisela brusquely by the arm. "We're going," he said.

"Oh?" She was startled, evidently wanting to say or do the
right thing but not knowing what the right thing might be.

"We're going to find Richard," he said.

"Oh, he'll be up in a minute," Dr. Klingman said.

"He will?" Edward stared at the old man intently, wondering if the remark was calculated or genuine naiveté. But the
answer to that came a moment later. Mrs. Klingman came
rushing in, flapping her hands wildly like a bird. "He won't
get him, I won't let him," she cried.

Dr. Klingman looked startled. "My dear—" he began, putting his hand on her arm.

"Let *go* of me!" She pulled free and confronted him.
"He'll destroy him as he destroyed her," she said, shrill, out
of control. "With his Nazi girlfriend. How can you let that
happen? Are you crazy?" Frantic, she rushed into the bathroom and locked the door.

Very quickly, Dr. Klingman led them both out to the hall.
"She's very upset," he said in a low voice. "I'm sorry."

"Oh, we understand," Gisela said quickly.

Did they? Too bitter to speak, Edward took their coats from the closet. "If it—" he began, but before he could finish his sentence, the door opened. It was Alma and behind her Richard, bundled in scarves and a heavy jacket. Looking at his face, the startled light blue eyes, the fair hair, the pale skin, unnaturally flushed by the cold, the frightened, suspicious expression, Edward for a moment had an uncanny feeling that he was seeing his former wife. She seemed to stare at him, not complaining, but seeming to say, Where were you? I was alone.

"I'm sorry, Dr. Klingman," Alma was saying, "but I just didn't have enough on me for lunch. I just forgot."

"Oh, that's all right. We can eat here," Dr. Klingman said.

"But Mrs. Klingman said—"

"Wow, is it *cold* out," Richard said. "It's below zero."

"Is it?" Gisela said.

"Yeah, boy, we were freezing." Only then did he turn to Edward. "Hi, Dad."

"Hi," Edward said, lightly ruffling his hair. He could not, despite himself, will any more open sign of affection. It was as though his wife were watching and urging him on and he resented the dishonesty of this indirect plea.

A half hour later, warmed by hot chocolate and grilled cheese sandwiches, the three of them emerged from the building. The sun was out, a harsh winter sun, glaring in its brightness. They walked along, Richard in the middle, a mittened hand in each of theirs. As they were nearly down the street, the boy said casually, "There's where Mommy fell out the window."

Frozen, Edward looked at Gisela. Their glances locked over Richard's head.

"There were ambulances and everything," he went on and continued with the story, as though he were reciting an account of the most interesting thing that had happened on his summer vacation.

Edward, unable to see, the sun was so bright, stared ahead, pierced suddenly, as he had not been until now, by pity for his wife who had chosen so gaudy and uncharacteristic a way to die. Taking his son to live with him, as he now knew he would, he would be taking her, too. He wondered if this was what she had intended by her death—to make their past together a part of his future life, indissolubly. There was no way of knowing.

"We turn in here," Gisela said as they reached the corner.

"Yes, let's turn," Edward said, his back to the building. "Let's go through the park."

THE CHESS GAME

The building loomed ahead of them, tall, blank, impersonal, its many windows catching the late afternoon sun. Regina turned into the gravel driveway, slowing the car while Tommy, slouched in the front seat beside her, squinted ahead. An old man was being wheeled down another gravel path by a nurse who, despite the blustery March weather, wore no coat.

"Is it for old people, too?" Tommy asked.

"Any age," Regina said. She stopped the car, removed her sunglasses and placed them in her beige lizard bag. "Age doesn't matter."

"How about children?" he persisted.

"No, not children," she said. "Though, maybe—no, no one under sixteen, I think." She leaned forward, straightened his tie and ran a comb through the shaggy blond hair. "Tommy?" she said hesitantly. "Listen, be good, okay?"

"Sure, I'll be good," he said, mimicking her. "What do you expect?"

"No, I mean, look, I don't know what your father will be like. Usually he's quite all right, but—"

"Yeah, I know," Tommy said. "If he does something crazy, that's—"

"He's not crazy," she said firmly. "Don't use that word. He's sick."

"He doesn't have fever," the boy retorted with a nine-year-old's logic.

"That doesn't matter." She opened the car door, glanced at herself in the reflection of the mirror, an attractive woman in her mid-thirties, conservatively dressed in a dark suit. To an outsider she would have looked like a mother about to attend a PTA meeting or a women's club luncheon. Patting her hair nervously, she added, "You have to be patient, that's the main thing."

The boy, wriggling out of the car impatiently, didn't seem to have heard her or, at any rate, made no reply.

"He's made remarkable progress," Dr. Wang said, smiling as he ushered them into his office. Tommy began leafing through a copy of *Time* while Regina sat on the edge of a bucket-shaped black vinyl chair, frowning, nervously fingering the clasp of her watch.

"The shock treatment has been a help, then?" she said.

"Wonderful," he said. "Really remarkable." He was a Chinese-American, a genial, imperturbable man whose smooth manner sometimes soothed and sometimes irritated her. She glanced at Tommy, but he seemed absorbed in the magazine.

"I've been so worried about it," she said. "The shock treatment, that is. For fear it might do something permanent."

He shook his head, smiling, and sighed. "There are such old wives' tales circulating about these things. Most people have the most medieval conceptions that may, of course, have been valid at one time to a certain extent but are quite outmoded now."

"Yes, I realize that," Regina said. She lowered her eyes

then raised them again to meet his. "I know you wouldn't use any method that wasn't reliable."

Dr. Wang smiled expansively. "You really need have no fears," he said. "Be assured of that." He leaned over his desk and regarded her intently. "It's been fascinating for us," he said, "to observe him, quite apart from the shock treatment and its effects."

"In what way?"

"Well, his peculiar mixture—the remains one can see of a brilliant mind, still often operating on a very high level. In chess, for instance. Several of the doctors play with him, including one or two who are fairly expert, and he beats them all. There's an analytical streak there that still functions, despite his breakdown—combined, of course, with frequent childish and irrational behavior."

Regina looked out the window at the panoramic view that, with its display of the New York skyline, looked almost artificial, like a painted backdrop. "He always liked chess," she said absently. Then, hesitating, she added, "I brought with me . . . I have a copy of the magazine."

"They're carrying on without him?"

"Oh, quite well, but of course Vincent was sort of—oh, I don't know, the guiding light in a sense behind it. I don't mean he was an easy person to work for. No one thought that, but he set a certain tone and without him—"

"A ship without a captain," said Dr. Wang smoothly. He was already, however, almost unconsciously it seemed, shuffling through some papers on his desk.

"Yes, in a sense," Regina said, flustered, trying not to show it but talking more rapidly. "Of course, the technical details go along all right. And many issues were commissioned in advance." She paused. "No, but what I wondered was, is it all right to show it to him? Not for him to do anything but just for him to see, to have some contact with the past."

"Well, there are no answers to these things, Mrs. Cardiff,"

said Dr. Wang. "One must play it by ear, as it were. I don't see how showing one issue would hurt."

She swallowed and touched one finger to her throat. "You see, I don't know. Perhaps he would feel worse knowing it *is* continuing without him. Perhaps he'd rather think he is indispensable."

He lifted his eyes to meet hers, but in them she read no expression. "There is that factor, too, of course," Dr. Wang said. "And in intellectual men like your husband that is a danger—the feeling of omnipotence, the threat to this—it must be treated carefully."

"Of course." Regina looked worried again. She rose to shake the doctor's hand, but he, remaining seated, said, "If you wish to discuss any of these matters in more detail, you might drop in, in say, half an hour? Right now, I'm afraid, I have a meeting I must attend." He glanced just for an instant at Tommy.

"I'd be glad to," Regina said. "You'll be in your office?"

"Is that my charming wife I see?" Vincent said. He was lying in bed and turned his head to greet them. A large man with shaggy, graying hair, he looked like a disheveled bear that had gone into hibernation.

"Of course not," Regina said, smiling. "What made you think that?"

"Then it must be some nymph from yonder 'orizons come to charm and bewitch the eyes of men."

"Could be." She went over, kissed him quickly on the lips, and then called, "Tommy?"

"Thomas," Vincent said. "Greetings."

"Hi," Tommy said in a shy voice. He stood some feet from the bed, staring at his father curiously. He still had the feeling that there must be something catching about this illness and that he had better not get too close.

"How are things on the home front?" Vincent said. "Are

you taking proper care of your mother, seeing she doesn't get into any mischief?"

"Sure."

"Women need looking after," he said. "I read today that Henry the Second used to keep one of his wives locked up in a prison to which only he had the key."

"Peculiar," Regina said.

"Perhaps it's a solution, though," he said. "Prisons for all wives."

"And the husbands would all be jailers?"

"Yes, why not? You would look lovely behind bars, my dear. But, of course, beautiful ones—perhaps a large golden cage, like a birdcage would be the best."

Regina turned away, twisting her watch clasp again. After a moment she said, "The weather is really great out today. Don't you want the blinds up?"

She walked over to the window and pulled up the blinds. The room was drowned in sun. Vincent blinked uncertainly, like a mole, and put up one hand to shield his eyes.

"It's an extraordinary view," Regina said. She was aware of the stiffness in her manner, the desire to make small talk.

"Yes," Vincent said. "Extraordinary. But then, everything is extraordinary here—the view, the weather." He pushed back the blankets. "I'll take a look," he said. He ambled out of bed, walking slowly with just a hint of unsteadiness. When he reached the window, he stood staring out, not moving. He seemed in a trance, as though for the moment he had forgotten about them.

"What's that building over there?" said Tommy, who had come to look also.

"Oh, that's another ward, I think, isn't it, Vincent?" Regina said.

He didn't reply.

"It's a ward," she said again. "That's what I think it is."

Still looking out the window, Vincent said, "You know, I

read once somewhere that if you dropped a pin from the Empire State Building, it would go clear through a person. I wonder how far it would go through from here."

"It's the fifteenth floor," Regina said stiffly.

"Maybe not very far then." He smiled. "What do *you* think, Tommy?"

Tommy shrugged. "I don't know," he said.

"You don't know? Why is it no one knows anything anymore? Have you noticed how frequent that expression has become? I think this generation ought to be called the non-committal generation." He started back toward the bed and slowly wrapped himself again in the blankets.

"You've gained weight," Regina said. "Your face looks fuller."

Vincent smiled. "Yes, I'm becoming the very specimen of physical health," he said. "It's rather boring."

"It suits you."

"Does it? I suppose I have an image of myself as the lean, ascetic type, but what else is there to do here but eat? It's like a ship—only meals mark the time." His face, for one instant, despite its fullness, had a hint of an earlier sensitivity.

Regina said, "I've brought you the latest issue of the magazine."

"Oh good." He looked ironical and hostile again. "I suppose they're carrying on brilliantly in my absence? No problem there?"

"No, well, I spoke to Ethel the other day and as a matter of fact, they're having troubles over—"

He waved his hand. "Yes, yes, they're always having troubles. Don't listen to Ethel." He waved the magazine in the air. "It looks all right. Nice print."

"There's that piece by Nielson that you worked so—"

"That's come out, has it?" He put the magazine down. "I'll look at it later."

Regina hesitated, then said, "They miss you."

This was the wrong remark. A bitter smile appeared on his face. "Miss me?" He spat out the words. "Yes, I'm quite sure they 'miss' me from the bottom of their hearts. Especially Maconeghy, having to take over and get a higher salary. He must 'miss' me a lot."

"They aren't only concerned with money."

"Aren't they?"

"No, you know they're not."

"Do I know that? I suppose I know a lot more than I realize."

Regina put her hand to her forehead. "Vincent, don't be this way. Don't be difficult."

He looked surprised. "Why not?" he said simply. "Surely, you're paying enough to keep me here? If I'm not allowed to be difficult on three thousand dollars a week, when am I?"

She said, "Look, I have to see Dr. Wang. I'll be back in half an hour."

When she had left, Tommy stood looking at Vincent, his hands hanging at his sides.

"What would you like to do?" Vincent asked, propping himself farther up on the pillow.

"Oh, anything you want to," Tommy said.

"Well, don't you have a preference?"

"No, I don't care."

"Would you like to read?"

"I don't know."

"You don't know! That phrase again! . . . How about playing pattycake?"

Tommy laughed and ran his hand through his hair.

"Well." Vincent smiled. "I got a clear reaction to something, anyway . . . Would you like to draw? I could have the nurse bring us some crayons."

"I don't like drawing."

"How about chess, then?"

"Oh sure." Tommy nodded eagerly. "Let's play chess."

"Very good . . . One moment and I'll get the board." He reached into a drawer of the bedside table and drew out a board and a small inlaid box containing the chessmen. They were larger pieces than normal, carved of ivory in the seventeenth century. Regina had given Vincent the set as a present many years earlier. One by one he set out the men, holding each one precisely between two fingers. "White or black?" he asked.

"White."

The began to play. Both of them took it seriously; neither spoke. Vincent took longer to make his moves than Tommy, who tended to think a moment then impulsively move a piece here or there. Yet it was Tommy who won the first game. He forced Vincent's king into the corner.

"I give up!" Vincent said, throwing up his hands in mock surrender. "You have me. No doubt of that."

They set up the men again; this time Tommy helped. The next game was over in less than ten minutes. Vincent began moving quickly, too, but each move led to a better one on Tommy's part. Studying the board, Vincent frowned and shook his head. "I'm afraid you've done it again," he said. "It's a good thing we aren't playing for stakes. I'd be losing my shirt." He laughed. "Not that I *have* a shirt to lose at the moment."

"Well, I've been practicing a lot," Tommy said apologetically.

"Evidently. Where do you go? The park?"

"Yeah . . . Or I play with Jimmy."

"You must devote some time to it. I never even learned until I was fifteen or so . . . Is it your favorite game?"

"I guess."

"Well, want to try another? I realize I'm not giving you much of a fight."

"Sure, I'll play again," Tommy said. He was sitting up straighter; pride and self-confidence radiated from his whole body.

The third game took longer than the two first ones combined. Both of them played cautiously and until the very end it was unclear who had an advantage. But suddenly, in a peculiar move, Vincent sacrificed his bishop and thus won the queen. Tommy, flushed with his previous winnings, took it good-humoredly. "That bishop move," he said. "Boy, you really had me there."

The fourth game was less close; Vincent won again. This time whenever Tommy tried one of his accustomed tricks, he found himself either blocked or demobilized. "Hey," he said at the end, when Vincent's victory was assured, "you're better than I thought." Then, realizing what he had just said, he stopped and added, "I mean—you're really good."

But Vincent only smiled absently at this tribute and imperturbably arranged the men once more, file upon file, on the checkered board. In the next fifteen minutes he won two more games, the last in only fifteen moves. As he made the winning move, Tommy put out his hand to make his move, realized he could not, that there was no move to make, and drew his hand back. After watching him a moment, Vincent sat back against the pillows. "I guess that's enough for now," he said.

Tommy said nothing; his eyes, puzzled and hurt, were still fixed on the board, where the delicate pieces remained poised in motion.

"Tommy," Vincent said, looking straight ahead, his fingertips touching in an arc that supported his chin. "That's an old trick. I played it with you so you'd know. Men do that in pool rooms, all over, not just with chess, but with anything—Ping-Pong, cards. They let you win a couple of games, and then when you're feeling like you're a pretty good player, they suggest stakes. Before you know it, they've cleaned you out. You've got to look out for that kind of thing."

"Yeah, I guess so." Tommy's eyes flitted with barely controlled hostility to his father.

"I just wanted to show you a lesson," Vincent said. "That's all. Now you'll know." As the boy still remained silent, he said, "Do you think I've done it on purpose, then? Just to exert power over you? That's what your mother would think . . . Perhaps there's an element of truth in it, but then, what's so wrong with that, when you come down to it? Everyone enjoys power. Dr. Wang, even your friend Jimmy, your mother—they all enjoy and use power in their own ways." He picked up the magazine Regina had left on the bed and opened it to a certain page. A few minutes later he looked up, and in a cold, formal voice, said, "I'm afraid I haven't been a great success at entertaining you. I wish I was more inventive. If I knew how to stand on my head . . . I did once."

"That's okay," Tommy said. "I'm all right."

"You're sure? Not just being polite?"

"Sure."

A few minutes later the door opened. It was Regina. "Sorry for being so long," she said, smiling. She was armed in her social manner again, poised and in control. "I had a nice chat with Dr. Wang. He's such a sweet person, isn't he?"

"He looks like an underdone egg roll," Vincent said.

Regina ignored this. She saw the magazine in his hand. "What do you think of Nielson's piece?" she said. "I thought it read quite well."

"Except that it's been cut to shreds."

"Has it? I didn't notice."

"Evidently. Who went over it, do you know?"

"Well, no, I don't." She looked a little alarmed. "I could find out, if you like. I could—"

"Don't bother," he said curtly. Then he smiled suddenly. "You know, I have a great idea. How about this? Instead of cutting in the regular way, which ends up nonsense anyway, why not do it the way Burroughs does—just cut the page in two and combine it with some other page? Maconeghy's always yelling for a new format. Well, that would solve the whole problem."

She said nothing but remained looking at him.

"Aren't I funny?" he said. "Or even amusing? What a pity. I thought you used to think I was."

Regina put on her coat. "I'll see you next week," she said evenly. "Probably the same day. I'll let you know." She bent down to kiss him good-bye, but, as she did so, he reached up and held her by the waist, bending her down toward him so that the kiss might become more passionate. Feeling Tommy watching them, she stiffened and pulled away. In Vincent's eyes, as he let his hands drop to the bed again, she read a peculiar mixture of a desire to humiliate her, cruelty, and, in some almost hidden place, a trace of genuine desire. Almost at the door, she said suddenly, for she had forgotten it until this moment, "You don't . . . mind the shock treatment, do you, Vincent?"

He smiled. He was putting the chess pieces back in the inlaid box. "Mind? How in the world could one mind? I find it delightful, a wonderful experience. You should try it yourself, Gina, one time you're here. I'm sure they would let you. It's very relaxing. For the moment you blot out the past completely."

"I wouldn't want to do that," she said.

"Wouldn't you? You're fortunate, then."

He remained staring at her with such intensity that she had to turn away. "See you next week," she called in a faltering voice. "Say good-bye, Tommy."

"Good-bye," Tommy said obediently.

As they drove out the driveway, the sun was setting. Regina said, "I'm sorry, I shouldn't have brought you."

"Why? I don't care," Tommy said. "He's just a freak."

She closed her eyes a moment. "Don't call him a freak," she said.

"What is he, then?" Tommy said sarcastically. "He's very ill, right?" he said, mimicking her.

"He's ill," Regina echoed. "That's right." She stopped the car by the side of the road and sat for a moment, staring over the steering wheel.

"I hate him," Tommy said suddenly.

Regina said nothing. Then in a low, flat voice, she said, not turning, "I do, too—at times."

They were both silent.

Then, pulling herself together, Regina started the car again. "What did you do while I was gone?" she said brightly.

"We played chess," Tommy said.

"Chess," Regina said. "Did you? Isn't that nice? Vincent was always so good at chess."

THE BABYSITTER

Rona had never been interested in sex. Her parents, both psychologists, presented her with all the best books at the earliest possible age, books with colored diagrams and coy descriptions, books that emphasized the technical or by-passed it entirely with pen and ink drawings of smiling couples covered by blankets. She looked at all the books but, to her parents' disappointment, never asked questions. Did she know it all already, they wondered? It was possible; children in the city were so precocious, so advanced. They managed to convert even her lack of interest into a sign of superiority; she was an only child and they wanted very much for her to be superior.

In fact, of all these books, the only thing she remembered was a series of three drawings. The first showed two dogs, one with its two front paws leaning on the back of the other dog. The caption read: *This is a dog. It is standing on another dog. This is called mating.* The second drawing showed one dog standing and another dog being held in the air about five inches above the first dog by an anonymous pair of human hands. This caption read: *When someone helps them, it is called breeding.* The third drawing showed a man lying on top of a woman. Both people were fully clothed and surrounded by drawings of hearts that emanated from them like flowers. This caption read: *When Mommies and Daddies do this, it is called love.* She liked the third picture best and tried to copy it as a Valentine's Day picture for her parents. They did not recognize what it was about and thought it was very charming. They Scotch-taped it on their bedroom wall.

When Rona was seventeen and in her first year of college, she began dating a boy in one of her classes. His name was Malcolm, he had a slight limp from having had polio as a child, and he lived at home in Queens with his married sister, Eloise, Eloise's husband, Harold, and their two children, Oscar and Kirk. One night Malcolm invited Rona to come out and babysit with him for his sister's children. She agreed. They sat in the quiet, dark house and watched color TV. Her parents had never allowed TV in the house. She had hardly ever seen it and watched it in dumb fascination, especially the color, which was neither true-to-life nor true to the color of Hollywood movies. Instead, peoples' faces were greenish or yellowish and there were random spots of orange and blue, not quite in focus.

At midnight Malcolm turned off the TV and they made love on the couch. Had he been less ugly or cynical, Rona would perhaps not have succumbed, but it seemed as good a time as any and these traits, as well as the anonymous setting, appealed to her. The pain was a help also since it prevented her from having to regard this as something enjoyable.

When they were almost finished, a key turned in the lock and Harold opened the door. Malcolm did not see or hear Harold since he was lying face down on top of Rona, having an orgasm. Rona did see Harold since she was looking over Malcolm's shoulder, eyes wide open. Rona and Harold

looked at each other for a few moments. Then Harold retreated and made some loud motion of rustling outside the
door.

"Your sister and her husband have come home, I think,"
Rona said, having thought it more polite to wait until he was
finished.

"Go to the bathroom, quick!" Malcolm said, almost shov-
ing her off the couch.

Rona went, feeling the wet ejaculation dripping down her
legs. She was surprised there was so much. She wondered if
the drippings on the rug would attract the attention of
Eloise or Harold and, if so, what they would think.

In the bathroom she wiped herself with some toilet tissue
and combed her hair. She put on some of Eloise's perfume, a
type she had seen advertised but found too expensive to buy.

"Wow, what a drag," Eloise was saying as Rona came out
of the bathroom. "Boy, oh boy, these people are—we should
have stayed home and watched TV. You guys had the right
idea . . . Was it any good?"

"It was pretty good," Malcolm said.

"We're dumb," she said. "That's all there is to it . . .
God!" She went in the kitchen. "Hey, you didn't eat the
brownies!" she said. "How come? Weren't they any good?"

Harold offered to drive Rona home.

"Oh, that's okay," she said. "I don't mind."

"No, let him," Eloise said. "It's dangerous to go by subway
at night."

"I guess," Rona said. "Only nothing ever happens to me,
isn't that funny? I've never been mugged or anything!" She
laughed and looked at all of them. "I guess I'm not provoca-
tive enough, it must be something, I don't know what. I feel
kind of insulted. Everyone in my neighborhood's been
mugged at least once!"

After that Rona began seeing Malcolm more often. All
their dates were almost exactly like the first one. They

watched color TV and made love on the couch, only Harold never interrupted them again. Each time, at the end of the evening, Harold offered to drive her home. Malcolm had no license and had never learned—never wanted to learn, he said—to drive. And each time Rona refused. She supposed Harold must want to have sex with her. It seemed an inevitable thing, the kind of thing she'd heard about so much. She supposed she would do it eventually, but she wasn't sure.

One night she said, "Yeah, why don't you take me home, it looks like rain, doesn't it? . . . Anyhow, this man's been following me home from the subway, it's kind of weird."

"How terrible," said Eloise. "Then of course he must! Who is this man?"

"Oh, I don't know," Rona said. "Some guy."

"Black?"

"Can't tell . . . It's too dark . . . Oh, he never does anything," she said.

"Still," Eloise said.

There was no man. Rona imagined Harold knew that, though she wasn't sure. He was a small, worried man, a journalist, and he had that tied-up mouth of a man who spends a lot of time doing things he doesn't like. If he had not interrupted them that time, she would not have thought of having sex with him. Now it seemed the necessary next step.

Harold found a parking space after a long search and walked Rona to her building. "Do you see that man?" he said.

"What man?" Rona said. She was wondering if he would be a good lover or perhaps impotent or maybe not even interested.

"That man that . . ."

"Oh him . . . No, I guess it isn't his night on," she said. She laughed.

Harold laughed, too, though a little uneasily.

In the elevator he stared desperately at the numbers.

"Ten doesn't light up," Rona said. Ten was her floor. She had the feeling he felt trapped. For him having sex with her was a necessary next step in some other set of next steps of which she knew nothing.

In the front hall she said, "Do you want a cup of tea or something?"

"Okay," he said vacantly. "Sure, I guess, I . . ." He sat down on the bench and began undoing his galoshes. It took him a long time, he went at it very painstakingly, and by the time he was done, she had removed all her clothes and put them in a pile on the floor. At the sight of her nude, he looked frightened. Perhaps he had really wanted, needed a cup of tea or whatever a cup of tea symbolized. But how was she to have known that? She had no experience in these things.

Harold was a painstaking lover. Rona felt he labored over her as he had over his galoshes. It was sweet. But afterward he seemed to want to talk about his wife.

"Jesus, why does she want another child?" he said. "Those two are enough. Who needs three? What if she just gets pregnant?"

"Is this your first adultery?" she wanted to know.

"Yes," he said.

She supposed that was why he felt he had to talk about his wife. He must think she expected it.

"I can still make you a cup of tea," she said.

"No, better not," he said. He put his clothes back on and left. She was almost asleep as he closed the door.

After that Rona often let Harold drive her home. Malcolm didn't seem to care. She tried to get him to leave soon after they made love. Otherwise she knew he would talk about his wife and that bothered her. She didn't like the thought of people being married, it seemed unhealthy. Complaining about it was like complaining about having lung cancer. All that every-day closeness seemed claustrophobic, the eating together every night, much worse than sex with the same person all the time. That, she supposed, wouldn't bother her. Why not one person? It would be as good as many. Or maybe not, it was hard to tell.

One night Harold was out teaching and Eloise was out at her women's lib meeting. Rona and Malcolm did not make love since Rona had her period and Malcolm said he didn't like blood. When Eloise came home, she was in an angry mood. Malcolm had said their marriage was going through a "stormy period." When Malcolm went out to walk the dog, Eloise said, "I should leave him . . . Why don't I? Christ, all those women have so much more courage than me. They do! They've lived through it."

"So, leave him, then," Rona said. She ate a handful of grapes.

"I always wanted to be an artist," Eloise said. "Why shouldn't I be? I was good."

"Be one, then."

"Only I wasn't good enough," Eloise said. "That's the trouble. He knows that, the bastard." She thumped her hand on the table. "You know what I really wish?" she said.

"What?" Rona said. She thought Eloise was overweight and was going to say something about needing to diet.

Instead she said, "I wish I could get a divorce from my kids . . . You know, that's what's so unfair. You can divorce your husband, but you can't divorce your kids. How about that for unfairness? Or if you leave them, everyone's down on you . . . Him I can take, seriously, I can. So he has his cruddy ways, I mean, so do I—but the kids!" She laughed nervously. "Hey, you think that's terrible, I bet, talking that way about your own kids, huh?"

"No, I don't like children," Rona said.

"How many would you have if you were married?" Eloise said suddenly, urgently. "What do you think's a good number?"

"I wouldn't have any," Rona said. "I'm not going to get married."

Eloise looked at her admiringly. "Going to have a career? That's great! See, your generation, they can do that."

Rona was not going to have a career, she disliked her classes but did not mind the fact that she disliked them. Her parents had both pursued their careers with such ardent success that she, their product, had been left with very little desire to do anything. However, she said none of this because she liked being admired, even for the wrong reasons.

A month or so later Eloise appeared at Rona's door one night. Rona thought she had found out about herself and Harold and was going to accuse her. But instead she came in and talked wildly about how she had finally left and put an end to it all. At first Rona thought Eloise had murdered her children, but it seemed they were at home with their grandmother.

"So, I did it, I finally did," Eloise said. "What do you think of that?"

"That's great, Eloise," Rona said. She fed her because she seemed very hungry and watched with some disgust as the already overweight woman stuffed herself with cheesecake and crackers and olives. She herself could eat all the fattening foods she wanted and never gain.

She pulled out the trundle bed from under the studio couch where she slept and made it up for Eloise. In the dark they lay side by side and Eloise talked about her life. Rona sensed she wanted to be comforted and caressed her round body, stroking her vagina until she twitched and lay silent.

"I can do the same thing to you," Eloise offered tentatively.

"No, I don't like lesbian relationships," Rona said, feeling that she must not have made this clear.

"Well, so, what do you think—I'm one?" Eloise said. But her hurt passed quickly. She had been rejected for so many things that she no longer cared if the rejection was for the right or wrong reasons. Drinking bourbon out of a juice glass, she said in the dark, "Harold wouldn't touch my vagina. He just didn't like to, it was odd. He said it was like masturbating. Maybe he was right . . . I don't know. He used to always wonder if Malcolm was listening to us—you know our bedrooms are so close. He said I provoked him, you know, undressing with the door open and . . . Look, what was I supposed to do? Malcolm was ten when our parents died, he told you, I guess, they had that car crash, so what should I do, I mean, where could he go? We didn't have any relatives. There was no place for him to go. Harold and I were just engaged then . . . Christ, you can't keep doors locked all the time. You know how tiny our apartment is! . . . Listen, I worry about Malcolm, too. He never used to date anyone. I guess he felt self-conscious about his leg maybe. Also he was sort of mother's favorite, he never got over that, with them . . . I was so glad he dated you, I guess he gets laid some times, doesn't he? He should, it's not healthy, I told Harold . . ."

She droned on and finally fell asleep. Her naked body looked vulnerable. It reminded Rona of those cartoons that show nipples as eyes, belly buttons as noses, and vaginas as mouths. She put a large man's shirt on Eloise because her own nightgowns were a size petite, which would have been too small.

In the middle of the night Eloise muttered, "Fuck it, fuck it!" and almost kicked Rona out of the bed.

In the morning she got dressed and Rona said she had to leave herself, she had a class. Eloise said, "Well, thanks for putting me up, huh, kid . . . What am I carrying on for?" She fished for a pair of sunglasses in her large dirty canvas bag. "There's so much suffering in the world, right? All those weird rotten little kids you see on those posters with all those diseases . . . Don't you think so?"

Rona thought she was getting a cold. She had not gotten a good night's sleep because of Eloise and all this talk seemed to her crazy, morbid. But she just grinned and said, "Good luck, buttercup!"

Buttercup was what her father used to call her when she was a child. She hoped Eloise wouldn't get in touch with her again and even thought of having her phone number changed or moving. She wished she would meet beautiful people with elegant lives. She wondered where they were and where they lived.

Malcolm dropped out of school and Rona didn't see him. Then, four months later, she met Harold on the street. He was walking along, a newspaper under his arm, frowning. Seeing her, he stopped to talk.

"Yeah, Malcolm's not living with us anymore. He thought I was to blame for Eloise. She killed herself, you heard that, I guess."

"Oh, how did she do it?" Rona said eagerly. The fact of death never surprised her, but she was always interested in the how of it.

"Pills," he said briefly.

Rona was disappointed. A gunshot through the head would have been more dramatic or, if not that, then something esoteric, gassing in an oven, maybe. But pills seemed to suit poor, unimaginative, fat Eloise. "If you want me to babysit for you sometime, I can," she said.

"I don't see this bit of blaming me," he said. "So, she was pregnant. I would've let her have the child. I thought it would be too much for her, that was all . . . Hell, she could have had an abortion, she could have had anything . . . Malcolm was crazy, he really was a crazy kid, he always had this thing about Eloise."

"My rates have gone up to three dollars an hour," Rona said, "but I'm free during the week most times."

She began to babysit for Harold. He was having an affair with an older woman, someone in his office and often, after their dates, he would make love with her in the living room. Rona would stay in the den in those times, usually watching the color TV. With the children she was indifferent, letting them stay up as late as they wanted and letting them do almost anything. She felt happy. It seemed to her that, as a babysitter, she had found her vocation, her avocation. Her own life had never had reality to her. Things that happened to her seemed not to be happening. Whereas the lives of other people were always vivid, highly charged; she felt they were her life.

Sometimes Harold offered to drive her home after the woman left, but Rona usually refused. She said she preferred going by subway.

"My life is so peaceful, it's strange," she said to Harold one night. He was taking his blood pressure to see if it had gone down after sex. "I must have a magic fairy watching over me." She laughed.

"How do you like that? Ninety over one-forty-five," Harold said. "Not bad."

"Do you believe in fairies?" Rona said. She was relieved Harold no longer wanted to sleep with her now that he had found this woman.

"Homosexuals, you mean?" he said. He unwrapped the rubber tubing from his arm.

"No, real magic," Rona said. "I do, sometimes. Sometimes I think I see Eloise's ghost in the den."

"Oh, honey, that's all crap, you shouldn't talk that way." Harold patted her affectionately on the shoulder. "Are you getting enough sleep?" he said. "You shouldn't talk in that crazy way, people won't know what to think." He put his hand on her breast. "Are you jealous about this dame, do you want me to . . ."

"No, I *like* to go home by myself," Rona said, putting on her wool hat. "I don't need sex anyway. You stay here with the children. What if they woke up? They'd be scared . . . I can take care of myself. You don't have to worry about *me*."

THE INTERVIEW

"You've changed a lot since I last saw you." Sitting in the wicker chair, legs crossed, Renata held the pad in one hand as she looked at the movie star and waited for her reply.

The movie star was staring off into the distance. She seemed to be looking through Renata, into some imaginary landscape of her mind. "Well," she said. "It's just—my life has become so much more difficult since then."

"Difficult? In what way?" Renata had picked up this trick—latching on to the final word in the sentence, a mild form of coaching for a reluctant interviewee. But now she herself felt reluctant to go on. It was the wrong time, she felt. Too late in the day. Next morning would be better. "You were happier, then?" she said, rubbing her hands together. It was cold and damp in the small studio.

The movie star smiled. Her eyes were dark blue, almost brown. "I guess no one's *really* happy," she said, "are they?"

Renata smiled. "Sure . . . some people."

"Are *you?*" It was like the movie star's old self to ask this question, to reverse the interview, part of her direct, impulsive personality which, two years ago, Renata had liked.

"Sometimes I am," she replied, feeling she was dodging the issue. It often struck her as odd that, although she made her living probing into the lives of strangers, she hated to reveal anything about herself, even when she wanted to, even with those people she knew well. "Let's continue tomorrow," she said, folding up the yellow pad and placing it inside her bag.

The movie star nodded. A thatch of dark hair fell foward on her face; she brushed it back. "It's not like I don't want to be cooperative," she said, "but I'm so incredibly tired. You can't imagine."

Walking toward her hotel—it was only a quarter of a mile from the building in which the filming was taking place—Renata found herself thinking of the movie star as she had looked two years ago in London when she had first interviewed her for the magazine. It was one of the movie star's first big interviews (she was in the midst of a major publicity campaign) but nothing of fame or its trappings seemed to have worn off on her yet. She had come striding into the room with a gawky, casual walk, wearing skin-tight jeans and boots reaching nearly to her knees, with hair flying. Even her beauty, which was so deliberately not glamorous—she had worn almost no makeup—had added to this impression. Yet already, although none of her pictures had been released yet, she was commanding a salary of over two hundred thousand dollars a film. She had laughed and joked, teased Renata about being in a "predatory profession," but with a good humor that was infectious. It was as though she was happy without realizing it, without having come to learn that there was anything else in life but happiness. Her boyfriend, with whom she was living, not in marriage, hung around during the interview and Renata had formed the impression of a somewhat reserved, sincere, serious young man, also not quite in tune with what was happening, or perhaps already learning to try and ignore it.

Back in her hotel room, lying on her bed, staring at the elaborately carved cupids on the ceiling, Renata thought that the best thing to do would be to sleep. Like the movie star, she thought, she felt tired, "incredibly tired"—strange the way they all used those expressions of exaggeration, as though reality was not dramatic enough to be described simply. She had arrived just the night before, at one in the morning, and had hardly slept in the interim. Being alone in a strange city always disquieted her.

She had two hours till she had to meet her father for dinner. They were meeting at a restaurant in the center of town. She had hesitated that morning about phoning him. It would have been easy enough not to. He would never have discovered that she had been in Rome; he was too busy; their paths never crossed anyway. But then she had thought, why not? It had been over a year since she had seen him. Some old curiosity, affection, possibly love prompted her, although she told herself hastily she should not be surprised if she ended up regretting the whole thing.

"There you are!" Guido, although it was he who was late, always made it seem the opposite by his boisterous, impatient manner. "What are you doing, hiding in this corner? You look like part of the scenery."

Renata looked up. He hadn't changed, she thought. His hair had been that shade of gray white for a long time now; he had always, as long as she could remember, been portly. But all in all he was still an attractive man, perpetually suspended in middle age; she could not imagine him old.

"You're looking well," she said.

He shrugged. "Do you think so?" He grabbed a waiter by the shoulder. "We want a table in the back," he said.

"Did you make a reservation?" Renata asked.

"No, but they know me . . . Don't worry about it."

Sure enough, a few minutes later, they were seated at a

table in the back. In the middle of the room was an artificial fountain spraying pink water.

"And you?" he said.

Renata smiled. "And me?"

"How are you? Well? You're a little thin, maybe. Thinner than before."

"Just a little."

"Are you happy?"

"Well . . ." Renata paused. It was a moment before she realized their conversation was somehow a parody of her interview earlier in the day. Probing into people's private lives. Was it more or less excusable if you did it only for money?

"What happened to that young man?" he said.

"Which young man?" she said, stalling.

"That one you were with the last time, the reporter. I liked him, very resourceful fellow. Very nice . . . Did he get his divorce?"

"Yes, but . . ."

"But it didn't work out?" When he wanted to, he could be direct, acute, so much so that it made her uncomfortable, even while she was being pleased that he remembered these details, that he took an interest in her private life.

"Well, not exactly," she said, toying with the heavy soup spoon. "He's still so involved—"

"With the past," her father supplied. "He lives in memories."

There was something curiously literary about the sound of that phrase to Renata. When he spoke English, as he was doing now, it occasionally sounded like a translation.

"We can speak Italian," she said.

"No, no." He smiled. "I want to practice. When I see you, it's my only chance."

Renata smiled. "That doesn't give you much practice."

"Not much."

They ordered from tremendous engraved menus. Renata

chose something expensive, partly because she knew her father would be insulted if she didn't, partly because she really was very hungry. He called the wine steward over and began conversing with him—he loved making a production of such things and did, in fact, know wines very well.

"So." He turned from the steward who was scurrying away, head bowed, the huge key bobbing on his chest. "And how are things in the States?"

"All right," Renata said.

"How was your mother's wedding?" he asked. Before she had a chance to speak, he added very quickly, "I would have liked to come, of course, but I was very busy at the time. The spring trade, you know . . . You liked her bridegroom?"

He was trying to be polite, but underneath Renata felt the trace of irony, as though, without having been present, he knew what it had been like. For a moment she felt a closeness to him, like something remembered about from the past when, as a little girl, she had felt an ally with him, going to expensive cafés and zoos with his mistresses and being forbidden to tell her mother about it because "she wouldn't understand."

"He was all right," she said. She added, "He exports pig bellies."

Guido laughed. Then, ripping apart a roll and spreading it with butter, he said slyly, "He's a bit younger than she is, no?"

Renata nodded. "A bit."

"Well, why not? It's all the thing here and in France—older women, younger men. Some say it's disgusting. So—it's disgusting. Men have been disgusting for years. Let women have their chance!" He smiled broadly and gulped down his wine.

Renata drank her glass down too, so hastily her face immediately felt warm.

"How long will you be here?" Guido asked.

"Only a few days," Renata said. "I'm interviewing a movie star."

"So, you are quite a little career woman now," he said.

She flushed. "No."

"No? I thought you were."

"That sounds so derogatory," she said, adding quickly, "perhaps you didn't mean it that way."

"It's not a life for a woman," he said bluntly. "Maybe for a few years. After that—a husband, children. *That's* what counts in a woman's life."

She tried to laugh and at the same time, although she had given up smoking, lit a cigarette to hide her nervousness. "That's just the Italian in you."

"Oh?" He looked amused. "And you are now American, a hundred percent?"

Renata hesitated. "Maybe not quite."

They parted at eleven. "I have to get up early, at six," Renata explained.

"Then I tell you what," Guido said, suddenly enthusiastic. "Where *is* this interview you are having?"

"It's in a studio on the Via Cavour," Renata said. "Right near the—"

"Yes, yes, of course, *I* know," he said. "Well, I'll tell you what. I'll meet you there tomorrow. What do you say?"

"At six in the morning?" She knew he hated getting up before ten.

"No, later, afterward. The interview won't take all day, will it? We'll have lunch somewhere. We can really *talk* then. Tonight it's been so rushed."

"If you'd like to," Renata began hesitantly, "it would be—"

"Fine! Let's call it settled, then. At one, one-thirty. I'll meet you there."

Walking back to the hotel room, Renata thought: He's

right. This is no life. Why am I doing it? Just for the money? But at least her job was interesting. She had a chance to travel. Most of the time she kept busy, avoided depression, avoided thinking about the future. When she was younger, she thought her mother's life was a failure simply because she was too dependent on her father. If only she had a profession, she had thought then, she would be freer. It wouldn't matter about his affairs. *She* could have affairs, instead of migraine and overeating and tears. But now the success of her own life in avoiding this particular kind of unfreedom seemed meaningless. Freedom for what? To wander to strange places and interview people she cared nothing about, to ask questions and get answers to which she was indifferent, to write articles she would not have read had they been by another person? One avoids one trap and falls into another. But she hated thinking her father was right.

In the morning it was pouring rain. Waiting near the bus stop, Renata hopped from one foot to another, wishing she had brought a warmer coat. Her umbrella trembled as though it might turn inside out any minute.

The movie set was empty. A few sound men were setting up equipment in the large hall. "Is Miss K here?" she asked, approaching one of them.

"Haven't seen her," he said briefly.

Sitting nearby in one corner, eating a roll and drinking coffee, she saw the director. "I've been interviewing Miss K for the magazine *Youth*. I wonder if she—"

The director was a tall, craggy man with almost no hair. He waved the roll at her. "Have a bite."

"No, thank you," Renata said. She stood with the pad in her hand, looking around at the set—a moon landing with blue saucers and greenish sand. "What do *you* think?" she said suddenly. "You knew her before. Would you say she's changed very much since she began making films? Do you think—"

"Changed? Of course she's changed," the director said, munching his roll. "Who *doesn't* change?"

"No, what I mean," Renata said, "was, before one had the impression she was carefree somehow, enjoying life more, and now—"

"Oh well," the director said. "Certainly. One is only young once."

At the moment the movie star's boyfriend walked by. He was holding a newspaper in front of him, reading. Renata went over and touched his shoulder. "Is Miss K here yet?" she said.

He looked at her, his face blank. He had long hair, almost shoulder length, and deepset, striking eyes with lashes as thick as a girl's. "You were here yesterday," he said. "Yes, you're the one we met two years ago who—"

"Yes, that's right," Renata said eagerly, pleased he remembered. "We all had lunch together then."

"Your article was quite good," he said, adding quickly, "for that type of thing . . . I must confess I rarely read such things."

Renata laughed. "I don't either." She frowned. "Would you mind if I—could I ask you a few questions?"

He stared at her hostilely. "About what?"

"Will you marry?"

"I don't know. We might. Then again we might not. Nothing is settled."

"But would you *like* to get married?"

"I would like an ordinary life," he said flatly.

"And you think that's still possible now with Miss K so much in the public's eye, so exposed to . . . so many different things?"

Instead of answering, he stared at her. After an instant he said, "You know, you shouldn't have a job like this."

"Why?" Renata said.

"It's degrading," he said. "You degrade both yourself and the person you are interviewing."

Renata flushed. "Well, it's a job."

The movie star was in her small cabin being made up by two men. A small bald man was penciling her eyebrows. A lanky fellow with a beard was holding out a lock of hair and teasing it with a small steel comb. "Could I—" Renata began, standing in the doorway, pad in hand.

"Ask away," the movie star said. "Ask whatever you want. But let's get it over with."

Renata sat down at the movie star's feet on a small red stool that was not very comfortable. She consulted the list of questions underlined in red by her editor as *very important.* "Do you want to get married?" she said.

"Marriage is outdated," the movie star said emphatically. "It belongs to the last century. I don't believe in it myself. Everyone who is married is unhappy . . . *You* were engaged when I last saw you. Did *you* get married?"

"No," Renata said after a moment.

"There, you see!" The movie star opened one blue eye as the little man began painting the other, and with it regarded Renata triumphantly. "In this century to be a woman is a problem . . . Not that I wish I'd lived in any other age." Suddenly she waved her hand impatiently. The little man with the brush leaped back, startled. "Can you imagine it taking so long to look 'natural'?" After a minute she said impulsively, "You know, you're lucky."

"In what way?"

The movie star looked dreamy. "You have a simple life," she said. "You know what you want. *I* was like that two years ago, I had what I wanted. Or at least I *knew* what I wanted . . . Or I *thought* I knew."

"Miss Soliana?"

Renata looked up at the woman in the door.

"Telephone . . . Down the hall."

It was her father. It was a bad connection. His voice sounded strange, unlike him. ". . . sorry, I just can't," he said.

"What? Can't what?" said Renata. She shook the phone as though it were a radio that was out of order and might be set right by a small gesture.

"Lunch," came her father's voice from what seemed like far, far away. "I have to meet Polialo, you know . . . out of town."

"Tonight, then," she suggested.

"I'm all tied up," he said. "I'm so sorry, Renata. Really. I wanted us to talk . . . Give your mother my best wishes."

"I will," said Renata.

"Next time we will have time together," he said.

"Yes," Renata said.

She put down the phone. With her hands at her sides, she stood staring off into space. Suddenly, uncontrollably, she yawned.

The director walked by. "You'd better have some coffee," he said. "It will keep you awake." He held out the paper container.

Renata smiled. "Thank you," she said and took a sip.

The director said, "At noon we will have lunch and I will tell you all about Miss K . . . I will tell you more than she knows herself. I will tell you everything."

In the café four hours later the director, biting into a large sandwich, said, "You want a happy story, no? That is what all American magazines want. Well, put this down. They will love it. They will eat it up, as they say. Say—" He looked off into space, like a man composing a symphony. "Say fame has changed her, but only in that now she wants more, needs more than before. Life has become more complicated for her, but underneath she is the same happy little girl she ever was. Say that all she wants in life is a home and ten little bambini, all in a row. Say—" He stopped, noticing that Renata was staring at him, but blankly, with a dreamlike expression. "But you are not writing," the director said. "Write! Write what I say. You will have a good interview."

Happy, wrote Renata in large letters on her yellow pad. She is happy.

PANSY'S DEMISE

"It was an affirmation of life," Lulu said. She sat down on the end of the sofa. "Well, don't look at me that way," she said. "It was."

"Lulu, you take it," Myer said.

"What do you mean?"

"For sheer unadulterated—"

"Unadulterated what?" Jake said. He was just entering the room, the bagful of coffee containers under his arm.

"Lulu is a crapologist," Myer said. He went over and took a container out without looking to see if it was his. "A specialist in—"

"All I said . . ." Lulu said.

"How is it an affirmation of life to kill yourself?" said Myer.

"In this sense," said Lulu. "In the sense that, well, if you're all by yourself and you do it, if you're just sitting at home or somewhere all depressed, and you just can't figure a way out—that's one thing."

"What thing?" Myer said.

"Let her finish," Jake said.

"It's another thing if you do it in the heat of the moment as it were," Lulu went on, unperturbed, "in the heat of *feeling* something."

"Rage," Myer said.

"Rage is a feeling," Jake said.

"You two are a wonderful comfort," said Myer. "I'm glad I called you."

"So, we'll go," Lulu said.

Myer grimaced. For the first time his tone softened. "No, stay," he said. "What the hell."

There was a moment of silence.

"The coffee is good, Jake," Lulu said softly.

Jake said, "You know, I saw Pansy just the other day, if you want to know."

"You *did?*" Lulu said. "You never mentioned it."

"Well—" He shrugged. "There was nothing to mention. We didn't even speak. It was in Macy's. She was going up one escalator. I was going down another. She didn't even see me, I don't think."

"And?" Myer said.

"What?" said Jake. He looked bemused.

"And what of it?" Meyer said. "What was the purpose of this bit of information?"

"There was no purpose," Jake said.

"God, Myer, you're in a bitch of a mood!" Lulu said.

"Am I?"

"Yes!"

He smiled. "Well, look, I mean, wouldn't *you* be?"

"No," Jake said.

"No?" Lulu looked surprised.

"Well, it isn't like it was anyone's fault," Jake said. "It wasn't Myer's fault."

"Wasn't it?" Myer said.

"How could it be?" Jake said.

"It's funny you'd say that," said Lulu. "I thought you believed in crime and punishment."

"But there's no crime here," Jake said, "as *I* see it. So why punishment?"

Myer said, "Men have more mercy than women. That's true. Pansy had no mercy either."

"I just don't think there was any crime involved," Jake said.

"But it might not have happened if—" Lulu stopped. "You know what I mean."

"It would've happened," Jake said.

"How do you know?" Myer said. He watched him carefully.

"It would've," Jake repeated.

"You think she was doomed?" Lulu said. "That's what you think?" She set down her coffee. "Mine was without sugar," she said. "You took mine, Myer."

"I drank it already."

"Bastard."

"It was inevitable," Jake said.

"It's interesting you say that," said Myer. "I mean, I've thought that too at times. But I was never sure. What's inevitable, after all?"

"Pansy had such a quality," Lulu said. "You felt it. Maybe that's this doomed thing. The way she'd look at you at times."

"Those eyes," Jake said.

"She had extraordinary eyes," Myer agreed. He smiled. "I married her for her eyes . . . Maybe I divorced her for her eyes."

"*You* divorced *her?*" Lulu said. "That's a new one."

"Correction," Myer said. "We divorced each other. A mutual act . . . With Lulu you always have to be precise," he said.

Jake said, "With Lulu you always have to be a lot of things."

Myer raised his coffee cup. "To precision!" he said.

"I love the way you both are!" said Lulu, pouting.

"How are we, dear?" Myer said.

"Going on that way." She stared out the window. "I just feel . . . bereaved," she said. "Pansy was my closest friend."

"Oh Lulu!" Jake said.

"She was . . . We were very close . . . So we didn't see each other as much anymore? That doesn't matter. You don't have to *see* someone. When we met we felt a certain—"

"Communion?" Myer offered.

"You make everything into some slimy thing," Lulu said. "You just don't believe women can be friends."

"I don't?"

"You don't believe in anything good or decent. You make everything sound all slimy."

"Defense, defense!" Myer cried. "Where's my defense?"

"Don't be too hard on Myer," Jake said. "Think how he's feeling."

"Well, he made her do it," Lulu said.

"How can you *say* that, Lulu?" said Jake. "*Made* her do it!"

"He did!" Lulu was flushed, excited. "I know he did . . . Didn't you?"

Myer said, "No, no, I did not, Lulu . . . I mean, I appreciate your attributing to me this grandiose power. I'm touched. But the fact is Pansy was upset when she came here. I said nothing, hardly anything—if I did, well, she provoked it," he added more quietly.

"Well, you admit it," Lulu said. "You did say things."

"Lulu, this is incredible," Jake said. "What are you accusing him of? . . . We were all fond of Pansy."

"He just goes around destroying people," Lulu said.

There was a moment of silence.

Myer said, "I guess I should have worn my Frankenstein mask tonight, played the part."

"He destroys people, that's all," Lulu said.

"Everyone destroys people," Jake said.

"*You* don't," Lulu said.

He said nothing.

"*You* don't," Lulu said again.

"Maybe he does," Myer said. "Maybe you just don't know about it."

She looked at him. "Meaning?"

He shrugged.

"Well, stop making all these enigmatic remarks, Myer! For God's sake!"

"I'm not the only villain around," Myer said.

"Who said you were?"

"We're all guilty in these things . . . all of us."

"I agree," Jake said.

"Well, if you want to shmush the guilt around," Lulu said, "make it all so vague, like, We're all guilty, all that Camus crap—"

"Don't you love Lulu when she starts talking about philosophy?" Myer said.

Jake smiled, but said, "Myer, come on."

"Husbands and wives unite! . . . No, I'm sorry, Lulu. In fact, quite often, you touch on the essence, the inner core of—"

"I don't know why you pick on me!" Lulu said violently. "We're not even married!"

"There you are," Jake said, laughing.

"I'm no worse than anyone," Lulu said. "Pansy was no angel either. I mean, I don't want to criticize the dead, but, like, Pansy often said—"

"What?" said Jake.

"Oh, nothing!"

"Oh, nothing!" said Myer. "That's not right, Loopsiloo. Out with it."

Lulu looked embarrassed. "Look, I didn't mean any *special* thing she said any *special* time. I meant just—she could be mean."

"Sure she could," Myer said. "Pansy was a devil at heart."

"Well, she suffered," Jake said truculently, not looking at either of them, "if that's what you mean."

"That's partly what I mean," Myer said.

"He thinks if you suffer that makes up for it," said Lulu, of Jake.

"Maybe he's right," Myer said. "Maybe it does."

"*I* suffer," Lulu said.

"You do?" Myer said.

"Yes! Over lots of things."

"Over and under?"

Jake said, "I don't know . . . There's something about this whole thing—"

"What whole thing?" said Lulu.

"The whole thing of sitting here, going on about Pansy . . . I mean—"

"Degrading her memory, right?" Myer said but without emotion.

"Right!" said Jake. "We are."

"No, that's true," Lulu said. Since no one spoke, she added, "But it's better to talk about it, isn't it?" Since no one answered this either, she said, "They always say it's better to talk about these things. It's no good to bottle things up . . . I know Pansy since—well, longer than any of you."

"Lulu has seniority," Myer said.

Jake said, "If you'll excuse me, Myer, that's just what I meant before, about being degrading."

"It was Myer who said that," Lulu said.

"It's the tone you use," Jake said. "All this squabbling."

"Oh Jake!" said Lulu.

"What?"

"You always expect people to be so high and moral. You set these standards!"

"Lulu has a point," Myer said,

"No one can meet those standards," Lulu said vehemently.

Jake seemed nonplussed. "I don't mean to do that," he said.

"I know you don't," Lulu said. "But you do."

"Well, everyone does something," Jake said.

"Pansy did all sorts of things!" said Lulu suddenly.

"Well, I'm sure she did," Jake said.

"I mean, bad things, too," said Lulu. "It's wrong to deify her memory."

"Who's deifying it?" Myer said.

"Well, Jake has this tendency," Lulu said.

"To deify?"

"Well, people who are dead, old sweethearts, aunts, and things."

"We all do," Myer said.

"I bet *you* wouldn't," Lulu said.

"You can't tell."

"You're too much of a cynic."

"Aha! But beneath that murky heart—"

"More murk," Lulu said.

"More murk to you." He grinned in a false way. "Fellas, I hate to break the discourse, but one point—do you want the stuff or not?"

"Everything? The furniture, too?"

"Well, the point's this. Either I call the Salvation Army and they cart it away, or you take it. I don't want it."

"She didn't have any family you might—"

"No," Myer said. "That is," he added, "I believe she wasn't on such good terms with them."

"But for the funeral and everything we should tell them," Lulu said.

"There won't be any funeral," Myer said.

"There won't?"

"Pansy always said she wanted to be cremated."

"How funny! In an urn and everything?"

"That was my understanding."

"Yes, Myer's right," Jake said. "I remember her saying that, too."

"Now, isn't it odd," Lulu said, "her telling both of you a thing like that."

"Pansy often discussed death," Jake said.

"She was obsessed by it," Myer said.

"Not with me she didn't," said Lulu. "She never did with me."

"Anyway," Myer said, "the point is, how about these things?"

"Give them away," Jake said.

"Well, I don't know," Lulu said, "some of her jewelry, maybe, I—"

"Lulu!" said Jake. "That's terrible."

"Why?"

"You wouldn't want to wear those things."

"Why not?"

"Belonging to a dead friend."

Lulu was taken aback. "Why? I'm not superstitious."

"It's not superstition. It's—I just think it's appalling. To even *think* of it."

"Well, gee!" said Lulu.

"Let her take a couple," said Myer, "if she feels like it."

Jake shook his head. "It's a repugnant concept . . . Anyway, you and Pansy were such different types. Her jewelry wouldn't suit you at all."

"Well, there's a totally different question," Myer said. "That's aesthetics."

"It's common decency," Jake said.

"I don't see why I wouldn't look good in some of Pansy's

things," said Lulu. "Not *all* of them. But I don't care. Give them away, then."

"I will, then," Myer said.

"There aren't any papers," Jake said cautiously, "anything you think—"

"I haven't looked."

"Now isn't *that* odd," said Lulu. "You think it's so awful to take any of her jewelry—it's just old crap anyway, she didn't have anything *worth* anything—but you'd go rifling around in her private papers."

"Who said that?" said Jake. "I never suggested rifling in anything."

"You implied if there were—"

"Well, there aren't," Myer said, "that I know of. So relax."

"We're relaxed," Jake said.

"Pansy wasn't the type to write anything down," Myer said. "She couldn't even write a grocery list. She was illiterate."

"What do you mean?" Jake said. "She was one of the most sensitive—"

"I didn't say she wasn't sensitive. I said she was illiterate."

"She could read and write," Lulu pointed out.

"I'm aware of that, my dear . . . I meant something less literal."

"Well, it amazes me," Jake said, "that you're still so bitter about her."

"I'm going to the bathroom," Lulu said.

Myer said a few moments later, in a quieter voice, "She told me you were seeing her again."

Jake just looked at him.

"Look, I don't care. I couldn't care less, actually . . . I just couldn't get all that crap before about the escalator."

"I did see her on an escalator," Jake said. "I wasn't lying."

"You implied it was the only time you'd seen her in months."

Jake shrugged.

"As I say, Pansy's private life was enough of a mess anyway . . . I doubt you added much more. I just wondered why—"

"I was in love with her."

"Were you really?"

"I think so."

"Aha! Equivocation!"

"Myer, Lulu's right . . . Why destroy everything?"

"Because I think it's a barrel of shit to say, 'I loved her.' I hate romantics. They're the most dishonest bastards on the face of the earth. Say you liked screwing her occasionally."

"Why make the rest of the world like you?"

"Because they are."

"Maybe not."

"Pansy wasn't someone to love . . . Look, I married her, for God's sake. I should know."

"And you didn't love her?"

"Sure, sure I did . . . in a way. But she wasn't the type to have deep, quivering feelings for." Disgusted he said, "Oh hell, look, have whatever you like. What difference does it make?"

Jake said, "Don't tell Lulu."

"Tell her! What do you think I am?"

"I mean, don't drop little remarks."

"Christ on a cross! Why should I? Little Loopsiloo has enough worries."

"I don't want to make Lulu suffer."

"Naturlich."

"It's a matter of priorities," Jake said.

"What is?" Lulu said, coming back.

Myer said, "Are you washed?"

"I am . . . You know, I'm hungry, aren't you?"

"I can get sandwiches," Jake offered.

"Corned beef on rye . . . with an underdone pickle," said Myer.

"Same," said Lulu.

"Beer?"

"Sure," Myer said.

"It was right out this window, wasn't it?" Lulu said after he'd left.

Myer nodded. He went over and put a hand on her breast. "Hi," he said.

"Hi," said Lulu.

Myer moved his hand to the other breast. "How're they feeling? Frisky?"

"What did exactly happen?" Lulu said. "She just came here—"

"She just came here, she was upset and I . . . said the wrong things, I guess. I went out of the room a second to get something, and while I was gone—"

"What things?" Lulu said.

"What?"

"Did you say."

Myer smiled. "Nope, Loopsi."

"Why not? Tell me!"

"I won't."

"You don't trust me."

"It's not a matter of trust."

"It was about Jake, I bet, wasn't it? . . . Look, I don't care. So it was. So maybe she was in love with him or something. Or maybe he, like, slept with her once. I don't know. Pansy was beautiful, so why shouldn't he?"

"Have some pride, Lu."

"Oh, shut up!"

They looked out the window together. He put his hand on her shoulder and began rubbing it, then moved it down her back. "How about a quickie?" he said.

She stared at him. "Myer, how can you?"

"Easy."

"But in the very room—"

"—in which you've been laid a hundred times before."

"But just four hours ago Pansy—"

"Lu, you didn't give a Chinaman's damn about Pansy."

She stopped. "That's true," she said. "But he'll come back
. . . He'll be back in a second."

"No, He won't."

"The delicatessen's right around the corner."

"That one's closed . . . It's always closed Sunday. He'll
have to go to the one on Second."

"It just seems wrong," Lulu said.

Myer said, "Close your eyes, grit your teeth, and it'll all be
over before you can say Jack Robinson."

"Jack Robinson," said Lulu.

"Hey, I'm not that quick."

A short while later Lulu said, "You're terrible."

"I thought I was pretty good."

"You know what I mean." But she smiled. "You shouldn't
be so bitchy to me when he's around."

"Why not? It's fun."

"He'll realize you're in love with me."

Myer laughed. "Lulu, you're great."

"He could've come back right in the middle."

"But he didn't."

"But he could've."

"Maybe he would have enjoyed it."

"Myer, come on . . . I'm going to wash up."

"The delicatessen was closed," Jake said, returning. "I had
to go to the one on Second."

"Same difference," Myer said.

"Where's Lulu?"

"She's washing up."

Jake walked to the window. He looked down. "It was from
this window—"

Myer nodded.

"It doesn't look so far down," Jake said.

"I guess it was far enough," said Myer.

THE GRAY BUICK

While he was making love to her, Larsen remembered the gray Buick. Distracted by worries as he had been of late, he could not keep his mind from dwelling, continually, on irrelevancies. This car was the one that for over a month he had suspected was following them. Her husband had threatened more than once that he would hire detectives to follow them, and now it seemed he was finally acting on this threat.

"Did you see that gray Buick?" he said to her afterward, letting a seemly space of time pass by from the moment at which she drew from his arms. With her in particular he tried to hide these preoccupations, although lately it had cost him considerable effort.

"What gray Buick?" Sara said, her eyes still closed, her voice low and tender, as though the question he had asked were of a more intimate nature.

"As we came into the motel," he said, watching her. "There was a gray Buick that followed us into the parking lot. There were two men in the front seat."

"I didn't notice it," she said. Slowly her eyes blinked open. "Wasn't it dark already then? How did you notice it?"

"It wasn't quite dark yet," he replied. "And I was looking for it."

"You think it's the same car?" Her eyes, fixed on his face, were caressing and in his present mood this distracted him.

He nodded. "I'm almost certain of it."

"Well," she hesitated a moment. "Even so, there's nothing you can do about it."

"I'd like to check anyway," Larsen said. "I may go out to the parking lot to see if it's there."

"Now?"

"I won't be able to sleep if I don't get it off my mind." He looked around the room. The motel at which they were staying for the night consisted of one large building and several small cabins to either side. They had rented one of the cabins, a one-room affair with a bathroom attached. It was a small room with a double bed, a rattan chair in the corner, and a TV set with its antenna folded in. Even the large box seemed to Larsen slightly ominous, as though it were following all their movements, recording what they said. "I'll be back in a minute," he said, swinging his legs over the edge of the bed.

"Don't be too long," she said. She reached out and caught his arm, stroking it.

"I'll be right back," he said.

He walked softly to the door, took his raincoat off the chair, put it on, slipped into his shoes without lacing them, and stepped outside. It was raining lightly, a warm late summer rain. He hadn't expected the rain and for a moment just stood at the door of the cabin, looking out. He felt cold and tired and wondered if he wasn't being foolish or paranoid. Still, as long as he was up, it couldn't hurt to check. Ducking his head, Larsen walked over to the front of the motel. The cabins stretched away from the main building like two long arms. In back of one of these arms was the parking lot. There were no lights, but his eyes were by now accustomed to the darkness. He walked up and down, looking for the gray Buick. He couldn't find it. His feet were wet. Once more he walked down a line of cars, peering closely at each one. There was a Buick, but it wasn't gray. Maybe he had been wrong about the color. Gray could look blue. As she said, it had been dark when they drove in. But he had been certain it was gray. He returned to the cabin.

"It's raining," he said as he came in.

"Hard?" Sara was sitting up in bed as though she had been waiting for him. Her dark hair fell loose over her shoulders.

Larsen shook his head, took off the coat and shoes, and once more got into bed beside her. "I couldn't find it," he said.

"That's good, then," she said, moving so that she was closer to him, her body touching his.

"Yet I was certain I saw it before," he said. "I could swear it."

"With two men in the front seat?"

"Yes, two of them."

She put her hand on his shoulder. "Even if it had been there," she said gently, "there wouldn't have been anything you could do."

He sighed. "That's what bothers me."

She leaned back, smiling. "The whole thing's a gag, anyway," she said. "He does it to be funny."

"Funny! Big joke."

"Sure. You have to understand his sense of humor. To him it's all a game, like some cops and robbers thing. You know— he's Humphrey Bogart, trailing the bad guys."

"We're the bad guys?" said Larsen, smiling grimly.

"Sure."

"You underestimate him," he said.

"You overestimate him."

He said nothing, but sat there, brooding.

"What does he care about it anyway?" Sara said with sudden vehemence. This was the tone with which she most commonly spoke of her husband. "He doesn't care."

"In his own way, he does," Larsen said.

"That's just pride."

"So, pride is a powerful emotion."

"Maybe."

"I want to be able to protect you if anything happens," he said.

"Nothing will happen . . . Really, don't upset yourself."

He said nothing for a moment. Then he smiled bitterly. "Have I become paranoid about this?" he said. "What do you think?"

"No, no, don't be silly."

"But what if I have?"

Larsen thought of the lecture he was supposed to give tomorrow at Bennington: "The Positive Hero in Soviet Literature." "Shouldn't I be a positive hero?" he said, smiling.

"No," Sara said.

"What am I then—an underground man?"

"Yes."

He shook his head. "I feel like I'm turning into one lately . . . 'Nervous, true, very very nervous, but why will you say I am mad,' " he quoted, raising one arm.

"What's that?" she said, looking at him, puzzled. He felt his moods disturbed her; she was not used to him this way.

"Poe," he said. Then suddenly he frowned. "Oh damn!"

"What? What is it?" His tone evidently frightened her for she put out her hand to touch his.

"My lecture."

"You forget to bring it?"

"No, no, I brought it, only it's the last paragraph. I said I'd make some changes and I forgot."

"It'll be good as it is," she said soothingly.

He shook his head and got out of bed. "No, I have to make the changes," he said. "I'll do it now."

"Now? But it's so late. You need the sleep."

"It'll only take a moment," he said. Larsen felt furious with himself. He had written ten notes to himself in the past week to remember these changes, and yet he had forgotten! It seemed a bad sign. Something is wrong, he thought, if I've become this forgetful. "Go to sleep," he said, bending over her. "You need to sleep, too."

She kept her eyes fixed on him, but worry as well as tenderness showed in them. "I can't without you here," she said.

"It will only take one second," he promised.

The radium hands of the clock showed it to be nearly three o'clock. Tomorrow, Larsen knew, he would be exhausted. This bothered him not so much because of the lecture, which he had given many times before and could recite almost mechanically, but because of the driving. He could let Sara drive, but he didn't want to. She went so slowly it always exasperated him. He found his briefcase in the corner, pulled the papers out, and carried them into the bathroom. Sitting on the closed toilet seat, he leafed through the set of notes. When he came to the part he wanted, he took out a pencil and wrote two new sentences in the margin. Just as he was finishing the last sentence, the door opened.

"Now you've got me worried," Sara said.

"About what?" He continued writing and didn't look up.

"Julie. I never called her."

"What do you need to call her for?"

"Just to remind her. In case he calls there, to say I'm staying the weekend."

"Oh, she knows the whole business by now."

"Sure, she knows, but what if, like, she's out or something? I should have checked."

Larsen finished the sentence and looked up. "You'll call her tomorrow morning," he said.

She was sitting on the edge of the tub. There was something both comical and sensual about the sight of her in her black lace nightgown, her round face pale and worried. "What if she's not in tomorrow morning?"

"She'll be in."

"She might have gone to visit Mother," she said, frowning. "She said she'd go one of these weekends. Maybe she decided this one."

He had been staring at her, bemused. "How beautiful your eyes look in this light!" he said, reaching out his hand. Then he put it down. "What were you saying, darling?"

"I've got to call her," she said. "I must."

"Don't worry," Larsen said. "I don't want to have you worried. I'll worry for both of us." Despite the lateness of the hour, his own fatigue, and the fact that he had made love to her less than an hour ago, he felt the stirrings of desire as he looked at her. Perhaps it was the harsh light of the bathroom that cast deep, mysterious shadows on her face. "Let's go back to bed," he said.

Sara stood up, pulling down her nightgown, which had ridden up on her legs. "I'm going to call her," she said.

He put his hand on her shoulder and slid it down toward her breast. "In the morning," he said.

"No, I'm going to call her now."

He clicked off the bathroom light. Once again they were in the dark cabin. "But it's raining," he said, still holding on to her as though he could physically keep her from going.

"I'll take your coat." She turned from him and he let his arms fall. The coat came nearly to her ankles. "I saw a phone booth outside the front entrance," she said.

It was only raining lightly. Sara walked through the wet grass, a pleasant feeling because her feet were bare. The neon sign advertising the motel blinked on and off. The Van Gogh Arms, it was called. She had imagined the lobby decorated with plastic ears. None of the lights was on except one on the south side. A girl was standing at the window of this room, looking out. Sara wondered who it was and decided it was a girl on her honeymoon. Already she's beginning to hate him, she thought, because he brought her to such an awful place, not someplace romantic and exotic as she had expected. Her own husband had taken her to Florida on their honeymoon, although it was August. He had said they could take advantage of the off-season rates. They had had their first quarrel then and he had beaten her. Later she had returned to the same hotel alone on a vacation and slept with the hotel manager. She had written him about it and when she had returned, he had beaten her again and broken her nose. She remembered going to the hospital with him and his saying to the man at the desk, "I just broke my wife's nose," and the man saying, "What are you, kidding? What kind of a joke is that?"

The phone booth was small and dark. It didn't even have a stool. Sara dialed her sister's number, knowing it by heart. It rang five times. While it rang, she stared out the window at the cars passing by on the road. She wondered at his having been worried about the Buick. She was not sure herself what a Buick looked like. One car was the same as another to her. "Hello?" Her sister's groggy, angry voice made her aware, suddenly, of the fact that it was very late.

"Jule? Listen, I'm sorry to call so late, but—"

"Sara? Jesus Christ, do you know what time it is?"

"Yeah, yeah I know. I mean, I don't know. I know it's late, though. But I had to call. I meant to try you earlier, but I thought—"

"It's three-thirty," her sister said. "It's three-thirty in the morning."

"No, I know," she said apologetically. "Listen, I really am sorry. The thing is, though, I'm going away for the weekend. And I wanted you to know if Harry calls—"

"I know. I know all that."

"I know you know, in general. I just thought maybe this

weekend you might be away. You said you might visit
Mother, didn't you?"

"Speak louder, will you? I can't hear you."

"Mother! You said you'd visit Mother."

"Lover? What lover?"

"Not lover, Mother! Oh come on, you can hear me, can't
you? I can hear you."

"I hear you like in spots, some time it's clear, then it blanks
out. Are you talking into the phone?"

"Of course I am. Can you hear me now?"

"Yes."

"Oh hell, it doesn't matter. Anyway, you are there. That's
what counts. You know what to say."

"Sure. Relax . . . Where're you going?"

"Bennington."

"What?"

"Bennington, Vermont. You know—modern dance, folk
singing, all that."

"Oh Bennington! I couldn't understand what you said.
Hey, isn't that where the Whosises live?"

"Yes, only we'll try to avoid them."

"And Jack Clark. I heard he was teaching there now."

"Is he really? Oh great. One more person to avoid."

"Wear your false beard."

"I'm coming as Lenin. I've shaved my head, too."

She shifted from foot to foot. She was beginning to feel
cold. Outside the phone booth the rain was falling more
heavily. "I better go back," she said. "He'll be worried."

"How is he?"

"Okay. I mean, healthy and all that, if he doesn't catch a
cold scrounging around looking for that damn Buick."

"What damn Buick?"

"I'll explain when I get back . . . Jule?"

"Yeah?"

"I really love him, you know."

"So? That's news?"

"No, I mean, oh, I don't know."

"Don't start worrying. It'll work out somehow."

"I guess . . . Anyway, thanks a million about this."

"Don't be silly . . . So long."

"So long." Sara put back the receiver but for a moment stood there, not moving. She glanced up at the lighted window, but the girl was no longer there. Mechanically, she felt in the coin return but it was empty. Walking back to the cabin, she went more slowly, hardly noticing the rain. She found Larsen in bed, lying on his back, both hands behind his head, looking thoughtful.

"It's all okay," she said.

"Good," he said. "Look, I knew it would be."

She sat down on the edge of the bed. "What've you been doing?"

"Brooding."

"Over what?"

Larsen hesitated a moment, then said, "Well, I just remembered there's a couple Eleanor and I used to know who live near Bennington—the Myersons. At least, they used to live there. I don't know if they still do. We'll have to try to avoid them."

"I can see I'm going to spend the whole weekend avoiding people," she said and laughed dryly. "Why did I come?"

He reached over and caught her by the wrist. "I wanted you to come," he said.

"Did you? Really?"

"Yes." He stared at her intently. It was important to him to make her believe this.

She smiled strangely. "Why did you?"

"Why did I what?"

"Want me to come."

"Because I love you."

"Is that a good reason?"

"I don't know if it's a good reason or a bad reason," Larsen said, "but it's the truth."

"But listen," Sara leaned toward him, her face suddenly urgent, almost pleading. "Maybe it just means you're a masochist, getting involved in something like this where there's so much pain and complications. Maybe we both are."

"No," he said. "I don't believe that. Some things are complicated. That doesn't mean one seeks them because of the complications."

She was silent a moment. Then she said, "Yet when I first saw you at that party, I felt I shouldn't go over to talk to you but I did anyway, as though it were out of my control."

"That's something different," he said. "I felt that, too."

"What is it?"

"Sexual attraction."

"Was it? Just that?"

"Why just?"

"No, but it was more than that, too . . . Wasn't it more than that for you?"

"Of course, ultimately it is," Larsen said. In his mind's eye he saw her as she had looked at that party at a distance of twenty feet, in a black dress, trapped in a corner next to her stout, voluble husband, her expression, as he had interpreted it from across the room, showing fear, wistfulness, save me! And probably she had been thinking nothing more than, This martini is too dry.

"It's three A.M." she said. "We'll both be dead tomorrow."

"Let's go to sleep, then."

"Okay."

Sara slid under the covers next to him. "I was on that side before, wasn't I?"

"Yes, do you want to switch?"

"It doesn't matter."

Sara thought: I wonder if we'll run into Jack Clark. Her

only contact with Jack Clark had been eight years ago. At that time, after three years of marriage, she had just discovered her husband was deceiving her with various women, some of them her own friends. Jack Clark had been a friend of her husband, a golf partner, and he used to come to see her and tell her elaborate stories of her husband's infidelities, giving full details. She was repulsed by Jack, but so desperate to find out the truth that she listened to everything. Finally, after this had been going on nearly a year, he confessed to her that he had made most of it up because he was in love with her. This had shocked her so much that she had insulted him terribly, saying things that made him stand and stare at her in terror. She remembered even now his face as she had said these things. Even after that, years later, when she would meet him by chance at parties, he would act obsequiously polite to her as though some trace of this former fear had never left him.

Larsen thought: I wonder if we'll run into the Myersons. He didn't see why they should. They might even be away somewhere or have moved to another part of the country. The last time he had seen the Myersons was just after his separation from his wife. He had stayed with them for ten days in their house in Vermont, ostensibly needing the peace and quiet of the country to soothe his nerves. Natasha Myerson came from a Russian family and stayed up until five every morning, reading Russian novels; she never arose before noon. One night, bothered by insomnia, he went into the living room and found her sprawled on the couch, drinking black coffee out of a mug as large a small coffeepot. They had a long, intense discussion about Dostoevski about whom at that time he was writing his dissertation, and by five in the morning he was making love to her on her husband's analytic couch. In the morning, at breakfast, bent guiltily over his coffee with Hans Myerson across the table from him, reading the *Times*, he was startled by Natasha who entered, yawning, and saying directly to him, "Love-making always makes one so sleepy, don't you find?" Every night after that he got up and "discussed Dostoevski" with her, and every morning her husband, who clearly knew all about it, was as calm and imperturbable as ever. He ended up leaving four days early, his nerves worse than they had been all year.

Sara thought: I don't care whom we meet. Let us meet anyone as far as I am concerned, even Jack Clark. Better be open than have this eternal secrecy. It was only for his sake she worried, his career. She didn't want to be a hindrance to him.

Larsen thought: Why did it matter about the Myersons, anyway? Let them see him with her. He would feel proud. Slinking around like this was absurd. But, of course, there was her husband and the detectives, her reputation—this bothered him and had given him more than one sleepless night.

Sara thought: Why am I so restless? Why can't I fall asleep? He was so quiet—sleeping already. He always dropped off like a log. Maybe he was not quite asleep yet. She wanted him to make love to her again, but she dared not wake him up. He needed the sleep. It would be selfish to wake him.

Larsen thought: Why is her back turned to me? Could he reach out and touch her there, near the neck, where her hair fell forward? He moved slightly, his hand poised, then sank back again. She would be exhausted tomorrow. There was no point in overdoing it. He must try to restrain himself, try to fall asleep.

On the roof overhead the rain pattered lightly.

When Sara awoke in the morning, the rain seemed to have stopped. Sun was streaming inside the cabin. She looked to his side of the bed, but he was not there. He must have gone to pay the bill, she thought. She dressed hurriedly and went outside. The motel seemed deserted. But the window where she had seen the light burning the night before was still open. The same girl stood at the window, but this time she was naked and simply stood there staring out, as though unconcerned about being seen. Sara ran to the parking lot where she saw him standing near a gray car. "I was looking for you," he said. He turned and it was then she noticed he was not alone. Her husband was sitting in the front seat of the car. "Yes, we're all going together," he said. "But I don't want to go with him," she said. The very sight of her husband terrified her. It seemed like a cruel and senseless joke. "Yes, you promised you would," he insisted. At that her husband got out of the car and the two of them forced her inside. They got in beside her and the car started to move. "I won't go," she yelled. "Let me out." She started to yell as loudly as she could, but no one seemed to hear her or pay any attention. Seeing the girl was standing still at the window, she yelled out to her, but the girl, with the same strange smile, simply turned and walked away, returning to her lover who lay on a bed in the back of the room. "Let me out," she cried, and this time began to scream as loud as she could, a high, piercing scream.

She woke up.

"Darling, what's wrong?" Larsen said, leaning over her.

Sara blinked up at him. "I had a terrible dream," she said. "I was so frightened." She could see his face only indistinctly because the cabin was still dark. Outside the rain was still falling with a light, pattering sound. Both the rain and the darkness and his familiar face comforted her.

"Do you want me to get you a sleeping pill?" he said.

"No, I'll be all right," she said.

"You're sure?"

She nodded and closed her eyes again.

A moment later when Larsen looked at her, she seemed to be asleep. She was breathing evenly. Perhaps *I* should take a sleeping pill, he thought. He got out of bed slowly, moving as carefully as he could so as not to wake her. He looked around the bathroom and saw his notebook with the lecture for the next day. Opening the cabinet, he found the bottle of sleeping pills. But there was only one left. That's odd. I know I brought more than that, Larsen thought. He took the one pill and went back into the cabin. It was only then that he saw Sara was holding a medicine bottle in her hand. Did she get up to take a pill? But I thought she said she didn't want one. Puzzled, he went over to take the bottle away from her, but as he did so, he realized her hand was icy cold. Carefully wrapping the blanket around her, he went outside. Not far from the door, near the entrance to the parking lot, were the two detectives. They were sitting on the grass next to a gray Buick, playing cards by the light of the flickering neon motel sign. He walked over to them. "There's something wrong with my wife," he said, bending down so they could hear him. "She feels very cold." "We know all about it," one of them said. "Don't bother telling us." "We'll take her back with us," said the other. "No, I'll take her," he said. "I can manage by myself." Turning, he ran into the cabin. To his amazement he saw Sara sitting up, putting on her stockings. She was wearing a black dress. "My husband died," she said. "You'll have to take me to the funeral." "But I have to give the lecture," he said. "There won't be time for both." At that she only laughed, a terrible, loud laugh. "Yes there is," she said. "You have to. You have no choice." She would not stop laughing. Larsen leaned over her, unable to stand the terrible sound, wanting to silence her once and for all.

He woke up.

"What?" Sara mumbled sleepily.

"What?" he said, bewildered.

"I thought you said something."

"No . . . I must have been talking in my sleep."

"What time is it?"

"Nearly six."

"We can get in an hour, then."

"Yes."

Larsen took her in his arms and held her tightly. "My God, what a dream!" he said. The terror of it still had possession of him; he felt he could not hold her tight enough.

"Was it a nightmare?" she said, her mouth against his neck.

"Yes . . . God, I haven't had a dream like that in I don't know how long."

"What did you dream of?"

He stroked her head, letting his hand run down to her neck. "I dreamt your husband died," he said. He didn't want to tell her the rest, about her.

Sara laughed softly. "Wish fulfillment?" she said.

"Maybe."

"How did he die?"

"It wasn't clear."

"Was I in it?"

"Vaguely. I don't remember that part too well. You wore a black dress for the funeral . . . like the one you were wearing when I first met you," he added suddenly, realizing the connection.

"The one with the bow on the side?"

"Yes, that one," Larsen said.

Sara turned her head so she could look up at him. "I had a nightmare, too," she said. "It's funny. As a child I had them all the time. I used to sleep with the light on in my room. But since then I haven't had them at all."

"What was yours about?" He kept his voice low and tender. He felt as though he had to exorcise for both of them the demons of the night.

"It was . . . it's hard to remember," she said. "Oh yes, it was about the car—the one you were looking for last night. You wanted to drive me and my husband up to your lecture together."

"The three of us?"

"Yes." She shuddered as the dream came back to her. "I screamed for help, but no one came."

"Poor darling," he said.

"I should have taken a sleeping pill," she said.

"But you did," he said, then stopped, realizing that had only been in the dream.

"You'd protect me if anything like that happened in real life, wouldn't you?" she said.

"Of course."

"Dreams are so terrible," she said. "I'm glad it's morning."

"I am too," Larsen said.

They got up half an hour early and packed. "We'll get an early start," he said.

"You don't feel too tired to drive?"

It was still raining lightly outside.

They walked toward the motel. Sara looked up at the window on the south side. "She's not there," she said.

"Who?" he said.

"This girl I saw last night."

"Oh."

Larsen went to pay the bill. When he came out, Sara walked over to him hurriedly and tugged at his arm. "Look," was all she said.

He looked where she was pointing. Two men were standing in the parking lot next to a gray Buick.

POSSESSIONS

Elvira Thompkins was a technician in Derek Wald's laboratory. The first week on the job she made a mistake costing the laboratory a thousand dollars. Apart from assisting Wald in his private experiments, it was her task to prepare media for the other three scientists. It was the media that she had prepared badly, infecting it with certain alien cells.

On Friday, as she was preparing to leave, Wald took her aside and said he was firing her. She was alarmed and pleaded to be given another chance. She said how much the job meant to her. Grudgingly, Wald said he would reconsider.

She had not been lying when she said she cared for this job. She could not have imagined a better one. Besides, this was her sole reason for being in La Jolla. She had grown up in Iowa but had moved to California as a girl to live with a maiden aunt in a small town outside Carmel. It was a town consisting mainly of retired and elderly people. Elvira had worked as a waitress in her aunt's boardinghouse and in the evenings attended an inferior women's state college. Her major had been biology. She had graduated this college in the spring and applied for a job as a laboratory technician.

The town in which Wald's laboratory was located was neither so small as the one in which Elvira had grown up nor so large as the one in which she had lived with her aunt. It was not a prepossessing place, but to Elvira this was unimportant. What mattered was that in this town she had a degree of independence she had never known before.

In her previous dwellings, at home, with her aunt, everything—the way of life, what she ate, when she went out—had been dictated by others. She had not objected to this at the time; not a rebel, she was a submissive, somewhat dogged girl who moved slowly, as though in a fog. But for the first time she had her own home—two rooms in the bottom floor of a white frame house off the main street—and her own possessions.

Her possessions were few—a lamp, some posters, a bright quilt on the bed, a phonograph—but at night, sitting and writing letters or reading, she would look up and regard them with pleasure.

"You've fixed the place up, I see," Wald said one afternoon. He was going on a three-day lecture tour and had dropped over to reiterate certain instructions to be followed while he was away. Since that first day he had not complained about her work. He did not praise it either, but he didn't seem the sort of man who would.

He was tall, heavy, bearish. Elvira judged him to be fifty or thereabouts. Someone said he had once been married. He rarely spoke, either to her or to the other three scientists in the laboratory. When he did he seemed abstracted or displeased.

She was pleased now and nervous as he praised or appeared to praise the decor of her small room. She sat in her rocking chair, the yellow pad in her lap, and looked at him, expecting he would add something more, his stare was so fixed. But he said nothing and departed.

Occasionally she saw him around the campus. Sometimes

he greeted her, raising a hand in silent salutation. But often he seemed not to recognize her and walked by without a word.

He taught her to play chess one evening when, after working late, they shared a sandwich and a beer at a local bar. Wald ate greedily—three sandwiches and two cans of beer. Elvira ate one sandwich and drank some beer. She was afraid it would give her hiccups and had been told this was impolite.

They played chess at her apartment. He saw the board in the corner, a present from her brother, an engineer who had contracted TB as a boy and married a nurse. She liked the way the pieces looked—small, intricate shapes on the flat board. He told her she caught on quickly. She was not surprised: She had always been quick at games.

After that they played fairly often, usually on Saturday afternoons when there was a break in an experiment and nothing for either of them to do. He didn't talk very much. He always won. Once or twice it was close, though.

He mentioned his childhood. Like her, he was from a poor family. He came from the south side of Boston, the fifth of seven children, six boys and a girl. The girl became an actress, he said. He showed her a photo. Of his marriage he said nothing except once, when he stumbled over the rug in the hall, "Women always like things around. My wife was like that."

"Children?" she asked.

"A son."

That evening he appeared to be drunk or possibly just more morose than usual. He said she should go back alone to the laboratory and complete the experiment herself. He would wait and read.

When she returned, he was asleep. He had spread the afghan over himself, one knitted by her grandmother, and was lying on the bed, facing the wall, snoring. He heard her come in, sat up with a start, and put on his glasses.

One evening he suggested they sleep together. The proposal was made flatly and not forwarded by any arguments or declaration of passion. In this Elvira was disappointed; she had believed that was customary. She asked why and he said because it would do both of them good. But seeing that she appeared reluctant, he immediately dropped the subject.

She had not been surprised he had made no advance prior to this. She was not a physically attractive woman and this knowledge was part of her understanding of herself and the world. She liked attractive things and people and stared at beautiful women on the bus, as she would stare at statues in a museum. Men she did not stare at; it would not have occurred to her.

They did sleep together after this, not the next time Wald mentioned it but the time after that. But the proposal in repetition gained nothing in eloquence. It was just that Elvira thought perhaps he was right—it would be a good thing and she ought to know about this aspect of life.

The experience was bound in her mind mainly by negatives. He did not whisper her name or any name, did not run fingers through her hair. Neither of them spoke at all. Afterward they both turned around and went to sleep. He left at two or three in the morning. They never had breakfast together.

They always went to her apartment. His was bare and disorderly—she had seen it once—with books piled in corners and dust on everything.

She found that after awhile the physical pleasure of the affair came to obsess her. But it always seemed to her a lonely pleasure, not unlike masturbating, which she had done as a girl when the lights were off and she was reasonably certain her younger sister was asleep. She imagined it must be different if you were married. Once, when they had fallen apart and were sinking into sleep, she said, "We use each other, don't we?" She asked it as a question, not an accusation; she wanted to know.

"Well, that's all human relations are, isn't it?" he said. "In one way or another."

At the end of the year Wald received a grant to lecture at a foreign university. He said he could get Elvira a job in New York or at a bigger university, but she said she would stay where she was. She did stay on for another year and then moved somewhere else.

Ten years later she saw him again. She had been married and divorced in that time and was in that part of the country to visit her in-laws, with whom she had remained friendly. She drove back to visit the campus and was surprised at how many new buildings there were.

She saw Wald outside the student union, which had been there when they were. He looked much the same—stouter and grayer, perhaps. With him was a woman with red hair who walked with a slow, waddling gait; Elvira took her to be pregnant. Ahead of them ran two little girls, one red-haired and one blond.

When the woman went into the building, taking the two little girls with her, Elvira went over and greeted Wald.

They began talking. He said he lived in Rye, New York now, in a gray stone house. The house, he said, had three stories and an attic and he had a study to himself. It had a brown leather armchair and a pipe rack with six pipes in it. He spoke of these possessions with a certain eloquence, as though he valued them, and when she commented on this, he said, smiling, "Well, as one gets older, these things are more important. The bourgeois comes out."

At this point his wife emerged from the building. Elvira wanted to say that while he had come round to her point of view, she had come round to his, for she had no things that gave her that pleasure anymore. But she didn't know how to formulate the thought and, anyway, his wife was then in front of them.

She asked when the baby was due.

MEMENTOS

Geismar had seen three wigs in his wife's closet once, sitting on the top shelf like decapitated heads with white featureless faces—one red, one blond, and the other a strange mixture of brown and white, like someone who had been caught under a painter's ladder.

Seeing Mari in the bridal outfit, the white gown swirling as she turned to smile at the buyers, he was reminded of this. Her hair was not her own—she was naturally dark and this was some reddish thing. Who the hell was she? A stranger.

The room was stuffy. He was the only man present. The women, to him, all looked too old to be shopping for bride's dresses. Or were they shopping for their daughters? They seemed nervous. Maybe their daughters, if they existed, were too ugly or marrying for money or marrying, for whatever reasons, the wrong person.

He was bored. He had taken the day off and now time was draining away. By three he had expected that they would be on the road already, a third of the way there. Of course, Mari always claimed she couldn't help being late. *They* set the schedules. *They* ran behind time. Still, it peeved him, as he

was peeved by the lack of ashtrays, the unopened windows—
it was a beautiful summer day out, for Christ's sake!—the
whispering, funeral parlor voices of the salesladies.

"Isn't that amazing?"

Someone was taken aback by a dress composed of what
looked to Geismar like transparent poker chips, held together
by chicken wire.

"It's a disgrace!"

The woman sounded angry, yet no one got up to leave.
But weddings are a disgrace, lady. Too impatient to sit still,
Geismar got up and left Mari a note, saying he would meet
her downstairs.

"If my girl comes, tell her I'm in there," he told the man at
the newsstand downstairs, pointing to a barbershop nearby.
They had met here before. The vendor knew what she
looked like. Settling into the shoeshine stand, he wondered
briefly if he set it up this way just for the luxury of saying
that phrase, *If my girl comes* . . .

He, Jay Geismar, had married too young. Just out of college, twenty-two he had been. He'd met his wife on a college
tour of Europe in his junior year. At thirty he had four children and debating moving to the suburbs to avoid the high
cost of schools and apartments. His wife was a rich girl, he
himself had family money, they had never been pressed for
anything they wanted, and yet in those eight years there had
been a sense of rushing, of getting everything done, out of
the way so that some long unrealized goal could be reached.
And when it was all, miraculously, accomplished, the children in the right schools, the house furnished by the right
designers, there was a sudden emptiness. Out with his wife in
the evening, Geismar would find himself experiencing the
bored irritation he had felt on a blind date. When would it
be over? And it was always with a slight sense of amazement
that he realized that he was supposed to take this woman
home, supposed to care whether she was in the mood to

screw, supposed to, if people even expected this anymore, love her.

His wife was a vapid girl and in the beginning this vapidness had intrigued him. She had seemed uninterested in clothes or doing herself up, uninterested in a career, although she had worked briefly in a Boston art gallery before their marriage. Jewish, she had gone to all the most Waspy schools and had emerged a half-breed with the values of the supposed enemy but at the same time a vague dislike for them for having made her feel an outcast for so long. He had taken his wife's blandness—a kind of terror, really—for serenity, had taken her quietness—stupidity, in fact—for feminity. In general had made all the foolish miscalculations that in retrospect a twenty-two-year-old might make. Though that scarcely excused it.

Of his two brothers he had been the only one to marry a Jewish girl, though their parents, well-known in New York banking circles, were on Jewish philanthropies galore. One brother had married a Catholic painter and divorced her. The other, a lawyer, had nabbed a plump Protestant who, like him, was interested in politics. His wife, with a tendency to self-congratulation that drove him up the wall, said it was a reflection on his "maturity" that he had not married "outside his faith." This from a girl whose only interest in a synagogue was the posh nursery school connected to the one near their East Eighties co-op!

For the weekend he wanted to drive up and get some things out of the country house he and his wife owned jointly. It was up for sale at the local realtors. His wife was "painting" in Portofino, his children were in camp or visiting relatives. Most of the house was garbage—a designer had done it—but there were a few things Geismar wanted to save, to make sure were not tossed out or burned in some primitive hate orgy. He would take Mari because he wanted company and because he wanted, for this occasion particularly, to feel

not only unmarried, but with a girl he knew his wife would
have despised.

Of course, that was an easy irony—one he would have liked
to avoid if only because it implied a certain weakness—to
date girls of whom, specifically, his wife would have disap-
proved. It was acknowledging a tie to her in reverse. He
should be above that. Above indulging himself by mentally
picturing her shock, disgust, displeasure, whatever! But, shit,
she *had* to suffer. It was just unfair, not the alimony, but the
bite taken out of his life by those jaws, a great bloody munching and chewing of *his* bones, *his* flesh. Suffering in Portofino
in her Pucci slacks with her divorced or unmarried friends—
yes, they had married so young they both had friends who
weren't even married yet!—sure, yeah, but that wasn't good
enough. He wanted despair! misery! the real McCoy. Screams
of anguish. All those Grade B horror movie effects. He
wanted his just desserts.

And would he get it? No. Would he get a part of it, even?
No again. Because his wife, God help her, God bless her, was
not a screamer. Even with four children, all those complications, the divorce would be arranged as smoothly and fault-
lessly as the globs of Dream Whip with which she suffocated
their desserts. She would not lose her cool. If, indeed, she was
anything *but* cool, one solid slab of coolness with just enough
blood circulating in the veins to simulate life.

"Was I a beautiful bride?"

"Terrific."

In the car Geismar expressed his annoyance at having to
wait so long. Mari was lying in the backseat, covered by a
blanket. "Yeah, no, I'm sorry. I thought I'd get out sooner."

For the rest of the trip she slept.

She was an odd girl, this Mari. Which perhaps suited him
since he had begun thinking he was fairly odd himself. She
was not beautiful, for one thing, despite being a model. With
her makeup off—and she scarcely wore any outside her job—

she was just plain, nothing special. Nor was she especially
sexy. She'd only had a few boyfriends, he'd gathered. He
would have said she wasn't that interested in men except
that she didn't like women either. Her mother was a school-
teacher, her father a Mexican Communist who'd lit out fifteen years before. Perhaps they got along because she really
didn't seem to care *how* he was, *how* he acted. Half the time
in bed they just lay there and talked or not even that. Curiously, instead of taking revenge on his wife by indulging himself sexually, he'd felt hardly interested in sex lately, almost
as though it were some taste that he'd let lapse. Did it matter? Did he care? Most peculiar, certainly. But for so long he
had tried to do the acceptable thing, even in this, that now
the only indulgence he had was in not bothering to put up a
pretense.

"Are you driving too fast?" Mari, waking up, sat in the
back, knees to her chin.

Geismar shook his head.

"Are we almost there?"

"Pretty close."

"I'm sorry we killed the day . . ." She put a hand on the
back of his neck. "I hate those bridal things . . . It's such
crud."

Geismar said nothing.

Mari said, "If I ever married, I'd skip all that . . . just do
it."

Geismar had sometimes wondered if she ever would get
married—she seemed so indifferent to it. She was the type, he
suspected, who would keep the baby if she got pregnant,
would relish that more than conventional matrimony.

"Did you like . . ."

"What?"

"I forgot what I was going to say." She lay down again.
"I'm so sleepy! Jesus! Do you think I'm pregnant?"

"I was just thinking about that."

"You were? . . . Big, happy, jolly thoughts about going with me to an abortion clinic?"

"No."

"If I had a baby, I'd sell it . . . Jewish babies are hard to get."

Yes, she was half Jewish—the schoolteacher mother, not the Mexican father. He'd only broken the mold that far.

"What price would you put on it?"

She laughed. "What a cynic . . . Did you think I was serious?"

"Yes."

"Well, I was."

They ate at a Scotch and Sirloin place just outside Huntington. It was almost too dark to see. Mari ate her own meal and part of Geismar's. She was always starving. Then she had the waitress put the rest in a bag. She liked to eat bones at night.

"This is it?"

"Yeah, what's wrong?"

"I thought it was a country house."

"It is . . . was."

"What'd you have, the Russian army up for the Fourth of July?"

The keys still worked. Geismar was a little surprised. He'd foreseen the lock being changed. No such luck.

In bed Mari fell asleep right away while Geismar was still traipsing around the house, checking things. One of the things he'd wanted—a scrapbook of drawings of ships he'd done as a boy—was right where he had left it. Why shouldn't it be?

In the middle of the night Mari woke him up and wanted to make love. She fell on him like a teddy bear, warm, cuddly.

"This is such a big, creepy house," she said afterward, her

head on his shoulder. "How may children did you have?"

"Four." He was sleepy now, hardly able to keep awake.

"Didn't your wife ever hear of the pill?"

"It gave her something to do."

"*That* type, eh?"

Was his wife a "type?" Geismar wanted to belittle her, even had a passion for it, but this irritated him. "You're a type, too, aren't you?" he said.

"Sooo! . . . Crabbiness in one so young?"

"Let's sleep, sweetheart."

"That's better . . . I like endearing terms."

They had a very nice breakfast. There were canned goods in the pantry to last into the middle of next year. Mari turned out to have an appetite for corned beef hash and gherkins and indian pudding. Even Geismar felt hungry enough to survive. After breakfast they lay around, talked, sunbathed in the back of the house. Then Mari went upstairs to take a bath. Geismar began looking for the other things he wanted.

"Whose room is *this?*"

He wished, in a way, she wouldn't poke into things. It offended some sense of privacy. Of course, why had he brought her? Yes, he wanted his past shared but in small delicate doses. He was to decide the doses.

Mari said, "Is that your daughter?"

"One of them."

It was a color portrait done from a photo and had a peculiar rosiness of the skin tones, peculiar because this particular daughter was pale and sickly.

"She looks just like me!"

"What do you mean?"

"She does! I can't get over it! Isn't that weird?"

"She doesn't look like you."

"It's so grossly oedipal . . . Jesus! I didn't know you were that type."

"Mari . . ."

"I know! Silencio!" She vanished to the bedroom again.

Geismar found the old bank books and the letters when he heard a voice downstairs. At first he thought it was Mari, having crept down for more food. But the voice was deeper, not a man's, but that of an older woman. He went to the stairs and peered down to the kitchen whence the voice was issuing.

It was Mrs. Fermillion, the real estate agent, a fat bull-doggy lady in tweeds, evidently showing someone the house. But it was Sunday! Why weren't these people in church or reading the Sunday *Times?* Where was their sense of ritual? It was eleven in the morning, for God's sake.

"Peter P. Perkins did most of the downstairs," Mrs. Fermillion was saying. "I don't know—do you know his work? He's very fond of woods, working in woods, you know, and Mrs. Geismar . . ."

"Mrs. Fermillion!"

"Oh, hi! Jay Geismar! What the devil . . . Now that is an odd thing . . . I thought you were supposedly slaving away in New York . . . How did you get in?"

"I had a key."

"Oh, of course, of course."

He liked Mrs. Fermillion—she was so unflappable. And a shrewd lady to boot. He ambled down the stairs.

The couple looked familiar. He didn't know them, but they had that look. He *could* have known them. She was in flowered pants and tinted sunglasses, he was square and distracted-looking.

"The Fields love your house, Mr. Geismar," Mrs. Fermillion said.

"We love it," echoed Mrs. Field. "We've looked all over—"

"They've seen everything," Mrs. Fermillion agreed.

"The blues in the living room are so subtle," Mrs. Field

said. She removed her round violet glasses and beamed. "So, so cool!" Then she frowned, scrutinizing Geismar. "Gee, it's funny, but I just swear I've *seen* you somewhere before. Now, isn't this awful! I just know it. Somewhere, oh, years ago. Maybe like on some prep school date or something."

"Yeah, well, it's possible," Geismar said.

"Isn't that the weirdest *thing?* Where was it? Where did you go? Lawrenceville?"

"Andover."

Mrs. Field smote her delicate freckled brow. "Now, *why* can't I remember? It wasn't—you didn't date a girl named Florence Louise Goodridge, did you?"

"I don't *think* so," Giesmar said.

"You'd have remembered if you had," Mrs. Field said. "She was this gorgeous girl."

"I guess I would've."

"Well, isn't this a remarkable coincidence," said Mrs. Fermillion. "Imagine your knowing each other!" To Geismar she said, "I hope we didn't disturb you. I mean—"

"No, I just came up . . . to get a few things . . . mementos," he said.

"Oh yes, of course."

"You can all stay for coffee," he suddenly blurted. "I can put some on."

"Well," said Mrs. Field, looking eager.

"I'll tell you what," said Mrs. Fermillion. "Let me just leave the Fields here. I have to run around to the office anyway. I'll come by in half an hour, how's that?"

"Sounds fine," Mr. Field said. "We're kind of bushed," he confessed when the lady realtor had departed. "We've seen just about every damn house in the district, I think."

"Well, you've *got* to," his wife said indignantly. "That's the only way to do it."

"I guess."

Geismar went into the kitchen and put up the coffee. He

could hear no sound from upstairs. Had Mari finished her
bath? Was she napping? While the coffee was perking, he
went back into the dining room to join the Fields, who were
busily perusing the ceilings and floors.

"It's sad," Mrs. Field said, "about your divorce . . . Mrs.
Fermillion told us."

"Oh . . . yes," Geismar said.

"It's lucky you have no children."

"Oh, I do! I have four."

"You *do?* Oh, that's right. It was the Turtons that had
none."

"We saw their house yesterday," Mr. Field explained.

"Four! Gee!"

"My wife's painting in Portofino," Geismar offered.

"Oh, she's a painter?" said Mr. Field.

"No, she just . . ."

"Say, listen, *I'll* get the coffee. You two stay here." With a
sudden alacrity Mrs. Field bounced into the next room. Her
movements were so like a bunny or some small woodland
animal Geismar almost expected to see a small tail attached
to her ass.

"You feel the property values here are . . ." Mr. Field
started when suddenly there was a clatter at the head of the
stairs and Mari's voice came down, piercingly clear, "What
the dickens is going on down there?"

Geismar looked up. Mr. Field looked up. There, at the
head of the stairs, Mari, naked as a jaybird, was peering near-
sightedly into the dark hall.

"We're having coffee," Geismar said. "Come on down."

There was another clatter and no more Mari.

"What was that?" said Mrs. Field from the kitchen. "Did
you say cream? I can't see the cream."

Mr. Field was still standing staring transfixed toward the
head of the stairs.

"Is someone up there?" said Mrs. Field.

"A friend of mine . . ." Geismar said, taking the tray from her.

"Oh, a friend!" Elaborately discreet, she sat down and sipped her coffee.

At such moments Geismar wished Mari was not just a bohemian slob but, at the very least, black—something to make little Mrs. Field bounce sky-high and out of this formerly pleasant Sunday morning. What were these people doing in his house! It *was* still his house, after all. Screw Mrs. Fermillion!

"I was saying we're glad the property values seem to be good," Mr. Field said, coming out of his trance. "In case one wants to sell later."

"Yeah, they're pretty good," Geismar said, thoughtfully stirring his coffee.

"Just pretty good?"

"Well, there's a lot of them moving in now."

"Them?"

"Oh, it won't matter to you. It didn't to us. They have their own clubs and the like. It's just it lends a certain . . . Look, half my business acquaintances are Jews, I have nothing against them at all, in *that* sense. It's just . . ."

The Fields were staring at him.

These people! Why didn't they say, why didn't they come out and say, Mr. Geismar or whatever your name is, you're crazy! You're a Jew, we're Jews . . . But they were scared. Scared as his wife might have been that, maybe, maybe he wasn't Jewish and therefore maybe he had the right to say whatever the hell he wanted, maybe he could refuse to sell his house to them!

"I didn't realize," muttered Mr. Field.

"Look, the property values will stay high," Geismar said. "Let's not kid ourselves. The economic climate being what it is . . ."

They were numb. They were too scared to speak. Even when Mari, clad now in blue jeans and a checkered shirt, bounced down the stairs, they hardly saw her.

"Is this . . . your daughter?" said Mrs. Field.

My dear woman . . . I am thirty-three.

When Mrs. Fermillion came back, the four of them were clustered solemnly around the dining room table, as though at a wake. The Fields seemed in a state of shock. Geismar wondered if he gave a damn whether they would now decide not to buy the house. Or would he just be discounted as a local eccentric. "Oh Mr. Geismar, yes, he . . ." Like Great Aunt Hattie going quietly mad in the ninetieth wing.

Mari said, "What odd people!"

"Yeah, well, they're a certain type," said Geismar, putting the cups back on the tray.

"They seemed so conventional," she said. "How can you like people like that? Is that why your marriage broke up?"

"I don't like them. Who said I did?"

On the way home in the car she said, "I think I'll get married next week."

"Who to?" he said, curious.

"Not you," she said. "Don't worry . . . No, there's this guy . . . I've known him a long time actually . . . We might make it together, I think . . ." She had on a wig and looked different, a beautiful girl but not very recognizable. "I'm not a romantic like you," she said. "I have a different view of things."

"Am I a romantic?" said Geismar. He was pleased in some remote way at hearing himself so defined. It seemed to give him a very coherent identity such as he had not felt especially lately.

"Maybe later you'll get over it." She spoke coolly, but not unkindly, gazing out the window, "but right now you're knee-deep in the past, like in a swamp."

This image he allowed to settle, to sit between them as they drove the next hundred miles into the city, the expanse of thruway opening up before him like a spool of thread that would never be totally unwound.

THE MISSED SUNDAY

"Then, why are we going," Preminger said, "if you don't like weddings either?" He was lying, propped up, on the double bed, leafing through the travel section of *The New York Times* and envisioning various fantasy vacations, skin diving in the Caribbean, mountain climbing in the Swiss Alps.

"We just have to go, that's all," Muriel said. Standing before the full-length mirror in her slip, she was holding up a shocking pink dress and frowning. "Will this be hideously gaudy?" she said.

"It looks great," said Preminger, "only, is that one of the ones where the hem is way up to your crotch?"

"It has to be," she said. "This is nothing. I'm conservative . . . I'll wear it then, what the hell. I hate all this bit with beige and colors like that for weddings. It's so funereal . . . Say, listen, what time is it?"

"Eleven-thirty," Preminger said, his eyes fixed on her body as she stripped off the slip.

"Oh Jesus. Is it really? Is it that late?" She pulled a bathrobe from the closet and threw it on. "Listen, Stanley, will you be a darling and take Evan over to Mother's? I'll never make it if I have to shower and all that."

"Okay," Preminger said reasonably. He slid his feet over the edge of the bed. "Does he have to bring anything special?"

"No, just make him take his windbreaker. He might not use it, but make him take it anyhow . . . And Stan, don't stay a million years talking with her, okay? Even if she seizes hold of you—"

"I swear," Preminger said solemnly, raising his hand. "I swear on all that is holy." He went over to give her at least a hasty embrace, but she was already darting into the bathroom and running the water. Sighing, he gave himself a brief glance in the mirror. He was a man of average height, inclined to be stocky, with freckled skin and ginger-colored hair. People had always taken him more for an Irish Catholic than a Jew. At the moment his nose and arms were sunburned because in his work as a sound man for documentary movies he had been assigned to an outdoor fashion show in Washington Square Park. His physical appearance never gave him unmitigated satisfaction, but still, he thought, turning away from the image, for a man of thirty-five he wasn't in bad shape. A pound off here or there might help, but still . . .

In his bedroom Muriel's nine-year-old son from her previous marriage was lying sprawled on his belly, reading a Batman comic. "Time to get going," Preminger said. "Arise, my boy."

"Isn't Mom taking me?"

"Nope, she's busy dressing. Got to hurry."

The boy rose reluctantly from the comic, then, glancing at his watch, said, "Hey, yeah, if we don't hurry, I'll miss Uncle Waldo. It goes on at twelve."

"So, grab your windbreaker," Preminger said. "Get a move on."

One of the main attractions of his grandmother's house was the TV, since Muriel barred TV from the house. The boy went over every day after school for a few hours to give

Muriel time to recover from her day and get dinner ready—
she was a receptionist at a large publishing house. On Sundays he stayed all afternoon and was picked up in time for
dinner.

The two apartments were only four blocks apart on River-
side Drive. Walking along on the park side with Evan trailing
behind him, Preminger felt abstracted. There had been almost no spring this year and even now, in late May, the
weather was gray and cool, overcast. Why were they going to
this thing? He had yet to find a really convincing answer to
that. He could see no earthly reason why Muriel's presence
should be necessary at the remarriage of her ex-husband. Not
only did it not seem friendly, it seemed downright perverted
somehow. When Preminger himself had gotten divorced
from Shirley five years earlier, they had cordially hated each
other's guts and sworn never to lay eyes on each other again,
and it seemed to Preminger this was the best, the healthiest
way to do things. This other way, with smiles and friendliness
on the surface and resentment and hostility burbling just
underneath—which was, he felt, the case between Muriel and
Sternbach—what was the point in that? Of course, with a
child involved, it was different. Some attempt at good relations had to be aimed at, though as far as he could see
Sternbach hardly kept up his end in that direction, always
being off in some strange place, painting murals in Mexico or
leading a group of students on some self-styled art tour to a
primitive Portuguese village. And why couldn't he have gotten married on a Saturday, for God's sake? During the week
both Preminger and Muriel worked, and even when he did
come over for dinner or stay the night, it was always rushed
and a little hectic with Muriel having to help Evan with his
homework and him still feeling in knots from the tensions of
the day. Sunday was the one day of total peace, for which he
had developed an almost religious gratitude. With Evan
away for the entire afternoon, it was possible to have long,

luxuriously lazy afternoons of leisurely love-making, lunches on the terrace—borscht with sour cream and fresh dill, beer —lying in the sun. Preminger felt these Sundays had a thera-peutic effect on his whole state of mind, He could face Mon-day and the routine of his work with a certain amount of fortitude.

"Hey, listen, Prem," Evan said, "are we all going to go out West this summer?"

"We may," Preminger said cautiously. "I haven't decided yet."

"Gee, I hope we can," the boy said excitedly. "That would be great, you know? Camping out and seeing the bears there. Where *is*—"

"Yellowstone," Preminger said, distracted again.

There, too, was a problem. For Muriel's sake this trip out West was ideal—all three of them together, giving him a chance to "really get to know" Evan, one big, happy family. But wouldn't it be nice, even nicer—this was his secret dream—just to put Evan in a camp—after all, he was old enough—and go off, just the two of them, to some idyllic, peaceful spot, some island somewhere, and just lie in the sun drinking rum and pineapple juice and have no childish chat-ter to listen to, nothing but quiet stretches of white beach, Muriel in a bikini . . .

They entered the small, stuffy elevator. Evan looked at his watch again. "Damn, I missed half of it already," he moaned.

"I told you to hurry," Preminger said. He rang the door-bell.

"Prem, how come it's you?" His possible future mother-in-law always opened the door without bothering to check who it was. In fact, Muriel had said, she never locked the door at all, despite the various valuables stowed away in the apart-ment, the art collection of her former husband who had died five years earlier. She moved aside to let in the two of them.

Evan made a mad dash into the living room for the TV set.

"Muriel's still dressing for the wedding," Preminger explained.

Mrs. Wallerstein made a disgusted face. "Don't *tell* me about that wedding," she said. "Just don't tell me." Although in her seventies, she was still a lively, iconoclastic old woman who played a vicious game of tennis almost every day with her park cronies, carrying a net out in winter and setting it up herself, dressing in black tights and sneakers and a scarlet loden coat picked up at a Third Avenue thrift shop, journeying to Washington on marches against Reagan. She was even attractive in a way, he thought, with her disordered mass of dyed-black hair, large, beaklike nose and sharp, amused dark eyes that missed nothing. She and Evan got along like two playmates of the same age and often, coming to pick Evan up, Preminger had seen her sprawled on the floor with him, building some complicated airplane hangar out of bits of slivered wood and airplane glue or giving puppet shows in which they would exchange roles as crocodile and alligator, each giving a remarkably lively rendition.

"Don't *you* like weddings either?" Preminger said, keeping his coat—he remembered Muriel's warning about returning early.

"Weddings I have nothing against," Mrs. Wallerstein said. "But that idiot—I wouldn't go to see him boiled in oil—or actually, maybe I *would* go to see that, but that's about all . . . Would you like to know the last time he sent alimony to Muriel? Do you know when? I know she doesn't like to talk about these things, she's too polite. And it isn't that he doesn't have the money. He has it, believe me, he has it. You know what his paintings sell for now? Five thousand dollars for one measly painting. Can you believe that?"

"Muriel said he was becoming more successful," Preminger said, glancing uneasily at his watch.

"Successful!" She gave him a scornful glance. "He throws a big pot of paint at a canvas and rubs around in it with his ass and that's successful. Have you seen those things? Now tell me honestly, is that a lot of crap or is that a lot of crap? Prem, you just don't know. You haven't *seen* what I've seen."

This was frequently her tack with him, as though he were some younger son who had scarcely emerged from the womb. She had always called her husband, a European businessman, by his last name, and the habit had stuck, only for himself it was more likely Prem than Preminger, a habit Evan had picked up from her. "I really ought to be getting back," Preminger said. "I promised Muriel . . . It starts at two."

She shook her head and looked at him sadly. Then she said, in a totally different voice, "You're going like *that*?"

"No, I'll change," Preminger said. "It'll only take a minute." If there was one thing he hated more than another, it was getting into a suit and tie, but in this case it seemed unavoidable.

"I'd love to see what Sternbach will show up in," she said wryly. "A court jester's suit, no doubt, with bells around his toes . . . Oh, that man! You know, I would strangle him with my bare hands, I swear I would. Do you believe me?"

"I do," Preminger said truthfully.

Impulsively she leaned over and hugged him. "Prem, you're a sweet man," she said. "I know that sounds terrible to say to a man, almost like an insult, but it's true." She gave him one of her devilish, mocking smiles. "If I were a little younger, well . . . Anyway, you know, that's the big thing now, and I think it's a great idea. Women and young lovers. Everyone's doing it now."

"A terrible idea," Preminger said, teasing her.

"You!" She pushed him playfully to the door. "You're a square, that's all."

He bowed his head humbly. "I admit it . . . Okay, see you later, then." He gave her a wave and started off, waited a few minutes for the elevator, and then, afraid it might be broken, went down the stairs, two at a time.

"What a place to pick," Muriel said, looking around. "He would."

They were down at Times Square, searching for the hotel. Already the sky was clearing and the air had become warm and muggy. Preminger felt his tie straining at his neck and wished he could take his jacket off.

"There it is," he said, pointing to a rather undistinguished-looking hotel wedged between a movie house and a rundown apartment building.

"It looks like some fleabag hotel," she said, "the kind you bring a girl to for an hour."

He took her arm and said jokingly. "Say, that's an idea. Why don't we—"

Muriel smiled, tightened her hold on his arm, and said, "I'm sorry about today."

"So am I," Preminger said.

"I just felt we had to come."

"But why?" he said, feeling he had already asked this question, unsuccessfully, half a dozen times.

She seemed evasive. "Oh, it's hard to explain. Just to show him that I don't care, that I don't bear any grudges. You don't know him. He'd get such satisfaction out of the idea that I just couldn't face coming. I want to show him he can go to hell as far as I'm concerned."

Preminger was not totally convinced by this argument.

"Anyway," she added with a mischievous smile. "I'm sort of curious to see what *she's* like . . . Aren't you curious about *him?*"

"In a way." In fact, Preminger felt he had a clear enough idea about Sternbach from all the stories he had heard about him. He would have liked to make him less clear, not more so.

"I want him to see you," she said, "to see us together, to see—"

"That's what I hate," Preminger said suddenly, vehemently, "the idea of being dragged forth like some specimen from the wars. Why should I be on approval with this idiot?"

"It's not on approval," she said. "Don't be silly. Stanley, don't be such a sensitive plant."

Preminger was silent, disgruntled.

"You're right, he is an idiot," she added, evidently sensing his mood.

They entered the hotel lobby. It was a large room with a faded beige carpet, a small desk off to one side, and a row of office-type elevators in the rear. A placard on a bulletin board announced: STERNBACH—GEGNER WEDDING: ORCHID ROOM, SECOND FLOOR. They entered the elevator silently, Muriel patting her hair in place, Preminger, his arms behind his back, staring moodily into space.

On the second floor there was another lobby, with doors leading off into various rooms on both sides. About a hundred people were milling around, drinking, smoking, talking. Muriel stared around the room. "I don't think I know a bloody soul," she said,

"Well, I certainly don't," Preminger said.

They wedged their way through the crowd to get a drink, discovered there was no more champagne, and accepted slightly warm screwdrivers instead. "You'd think they could at *least* get enough champagne," Muriel said. "I mean, even if it's American champagne."

"I don't like champagne," Preminger said.

But she was not listening. Already she seemed to him to have a distracted air, gazing this way and that, a vague, social smile hovering on her face. "Oh God," she said. "There's his mother." She turned abruptly in the other direction. "Don't let her see me," she said.

"Look, you're bound to run into all the relatives," Preminger said. "What do you expect?"

"I guess." She looked wistful. "I didn't think there'd be this *many* people. I mean, isn't there some etiquette for second marriages? You don't have as many?"

"I don't know," Preminger said.

"Not that he'd bother with etiquette," she said. "Still . . ." She raised her paper cup and clinked it against his. "To weddings," she said.

"Even second ones?" Preminger smiled.

"Even those." She smiled at him, her eyes warm and tender-looking. At such moments Preminger felt a sudden injection of good spirits, as though he had drunk a carafe of fresh orange juice on a hot day. But then, lowering her voice, Muriel whispered, "Listen, I heard someone say they're in Room 606 getting ready. Why don't we go say hello? We'll never see them afterward with this mob."

"I don't know," Preminger said, his good spirits vanishing as rapidly as they had come. "Do you think we should? They—"

"The elevators are down there," she said, ignoring this. "Come on, let's. It'll be fun . . . I wonder if he's shaved off his beard. I guess probably he has. The relatives would die if he didn't."

Room 606 was at one end of a long corridor, carpeted in a mottled green color. Muriel tapped lightly on the door and, before any reply had come from the other side, pushed the door open. Preminger followed.

It was a large room, cluttered with various overstuffed chairs and sofas. In the middle of the room stood the bride in her long, white dress, being pinned and stitched in place. She was a blonde, a nice enough looking girl, Preminger thought, with harlequin eyeglasses and a worried, almost tearful expression. In the corner, in one of the chairs, sat a man whom

Preminger assumed to be Sternbach, though he was, as Muriel had predicted, minus the beard. He was a tall, hefty man, slouched down in the chair with a bored, even disgusted look on his face. He had red hair a shade darker than Preminger's own and a long, horse-like face, a big nose, and dark, penetrating eyes that flitted restlessly around the room. Seeing them enter, his face lit up.

"Hey! Muriel! Great!" As she walked over toward his chair, he reached out a hand and whacked her on the behind. "You're looking terrific, kid. That's a great dress."

Muriel smiled and looked disapproving, but Preminger could tell she was pleased. "Abe, this is Stanley Preminger," she said, reaching behind her for Preminger as though he were an awkward child being brought before adults. "Stanley, Abe."

"So, this is Preminger. Well, it's about time we met," Sternbach said, giving him a friendly grin. "You're the man I've heard so much about."

Heard about? Preminger wondered. From whom? What? Immediately he felt suspicious and looked at the man warily.

Sternbach waved toward the bride. "And this zaftig female in the middle of the room, in case you haven't guessed, is my bride-to-be, Beverly. And the equally resplendent creature beside her is her mother, Mrs. Gegner."

Mrs. Gegner, a petite woman in her fifties with tinted blond hair and an expression as worried as her daughter's, gave Muriel a quick, not overly friendly smile. "Hello, Muriel," Beverly said in a slow, amiable voice. "I'm glad you could come."

"What a lovely dress," Muriel said, smiling in a way Preminger detected as her "social secretary" manner. "Is it peau de soie?"

"Satin," Beverly said stiffly, standing at attention.

Mrs. Gegner shook her head and stepped back to survey

her daughter from a distance. "Will you look at that?" she said, clucking. "Can you imagine? She's lost five pounds, just since the fitting. I don't know *what* we're going to do. It just *hangs* on her."

"It's worry," Sternbach said cheerfully. "Already she's worrying. Murie, remember how you swelled up on the honeymoon? Fifteen pounds she gained out of worry. After one week people were saying, What're you—pregnant already? They couldn't believe we were newlyweds."

Mrs. Gegner shot him a glance that could have killed, but he seemed unruffled. "Look at me," he mourned, turning again to Muriel and Preminger. "They've shaved me. They've taken away my manhood."

"You'll survive," Muriel said. "Can't you grow it back?"

"Grow it back! Sure I can grow it back, but a beard like that takes *years* of growing. It's not just the amount of hair or the trim. It's like a fine wine—it needs to age, to fill out, to gain a certain stature, a certain authority." He slouched in the chair again. "I feel like Samson," he said. "Look at me, weak as a baby."

"You look much better without it," Mrs. Gegner said firmly. "That's nonsense."

Sternbach shook his head. "Listen to that. Treason. High treason."

Mrs. Gegner turned to Preminger. "Before this you couldn't see his face," she said. "It was like some big *growth* covering everything. Now I can see if a man has, maybe, a weak chin, you know, something of that nature, maybe a beard will add a little something, but look at his chin. He has all the chin you could want. What does he need with a beard?"

Sternbach sighed. "Oh women," he said. "It's not a mere physical matter. It's a thing of the spirit, of the soul . . ." To Preminger he said, "You can understand that, can't you?"

"I've never had a beard," Preminger confessed hesitantly.

"See!" said Mrs. Gegner. "That's what I mean. What do you need with a beard in this day and age?"

Sternbach looked gloomy. "No one understands." Then suddenly his mood changed. "Say, how's it going down there?" he said. "Everything okay? No mob violence?"

"No, it's fine," Muriel said. "They're all eating away . . . There's no more champagne left," she added, with what Preminger thought was a slightly mischievous smile.

Mrs. Gegner shook her head again. Her mouth stuffed with pins, she muttered, "I *told* your father, Beverly. You heard me. I said, For a crowd this size you need ten gallons. 'Ten gallons?' he said. 'What do you mean? You having the Red Army? Six is plenty.' " She sighed heavily.

"The food is great, though," Preminger said to cheer her up.

"Is it?" Sternbach looked at him with sudden interest. "What do they have—little hot meat patties and things like that?"

"Sure, and lox and caviarish things," Muriel said.

Sternbach sighed deeply. "Oh God, don't tell me anymore. I'm ravenous." He looked at his watch. "When is this blasted ceremony going to start?"

Mrs. Gegner said stiffly, "It will *start* when Beverly is pinned."

"Pinned! I can pass out from sheer starvation by then . . . Say, Murie, could you do me a great, everlasting favor? Grab a plate and bring a bunch of hors d'oeuvres up here, okay? Just anything you see."

"Abe," Mrs. Gegner said. "Now you can wait until after the ceremony."

"I can't," Sternbach wailed. "I would if I could, but look at me, I'm weak, I'm pale—you don't want to have to carry me down the aisle in your arms, do you, Sophie?"

"All right, well, we'll bring up a few things," Muriel said. "Anyone else want anything? Any other orders?"

There was a moment of silence. Then Beverly said in a timid voice, "I'll have a meat pattie, too, if you can find one."

"Beverly!" came Mrs. Gegner's disapproving voice as they closed the door behind them. "You're getting just like *him*."

In the hall, once they had gotten out of earshot, Muriel said, shaking her head, "He's just the same. He certainly hasn't reformed . . . What did you think of her?"

"She has a nice figure," Preminger said absently.

"Did you think so? I guess she did in a certain sense. But why does she have to wear those awful glasses for her wedding? You'd think she could get contacts or something . . . It's funny how he always picks these upright, virginal types—I wonder why. It's not really his type. Maybe so he'll have someone to shock more easily."

"But you weren't upright and virginal," Preminger said. "Were you?"

"Yes, I was," said Muriel. "You'd have been surprised. I never wore makeup, I was as prim and straitlaced as they come." She gave him a teasing smile. "I wasn't always the loose woman you know today."

They got into the elevator, Preminger brooding upon this new, unexpected image of the pre-Sternbach Muriel, perhaps as she had been in her wedding photo, which still stood upon her bedroom bureau—dark, slim, serious, squinting at the camera, a vague smile on her face, a glass of champagne in one hand, with Sternbach in a brightly plaided jacket and red tie, his beard making him look like some Hebrew prophet gone Bohemian.

They shoved their way into the crowded room and filled a paper plate with hors d'oeuvres. But as they were waiting in front of the elevator to go up again, the elevator door opened and Sternbach appeared. Seeing them, he said, "Listen, folks, no time for food. The ceremony's starting in a few minutes." He grabbed a few meat patties and stuffed them into his mouth. "Umm—not bad," he said. "Find me a woman that will compare to a good meat pattie and I'll find you the answer to a man's salvation." He leaned over and lowered his voice. "What am I doing, getting married? Will you tell me that? Marriage is for the birds. I don't know what's wrong with me." He gave Preminger a knowing smile. "You two have got the right idea. Live together. Have an affair. Keep a harem—anything but marriage." As he darted around the corner, he yelled back at Preminger, "Keep a harem!"

Muriel glared after him. "What a thing to say on your wedding day!" she said. "How terrible."

Preminger put his arm around her. "Why do you take him so seriously? He just does it to get your goat."

She sighed. "I guess . . . You'd think he could at least calm down for one day."

He smiled at her teasingly. "Anyway, maybe he's got an idea."

To his amazement tears appeared in her eyes. "Stanley, don't," she said. "Don't be like him. Don't."

Preminger tighened his hold on her. "Of course not," he said gently. "I was just joking."

But as they went in to join the others for the ceremony, her face remained grave and abstracted, her lips compressed into a severe line.

The ceremony did not take long. There was a large room fixed up as a chapel, air-conditioned, with slabs of stained glass windows on both sides. These windows, by a switch, could be reversed into buffet tables, if room was lacking. The noise level continued almost unabated, what with the singing from the balcony—a voluptuous brunette with Turkish eyes crooning, "This Is My Beloved" and the baying of the two cantors who sounded, Preminger thought, like a pair of coyotes lost in the wilderness. The bride had to descend alone from a stairway, spotlights on her face, and as she did, Preminger saw her clutch the banister for support. She looked as though she might faint at any moment and, although a vague smile hovered on her face, it looked as though even that might be suddenly replaced by a rain of tears. Sitting in the first row, Preminger had a clear view of the bride and groom as they said their vows. The bride's Uncle Max delivered a short sermon beforehand on the virtues and physical beauty of the couple about to be united in holy matrimony. Sternbach kept mugging throughout this, and when the rabbi came to *Be obedient* he gave a broad wink at no one in particular.

Afterward everyone was herded into a large room. Preminger, who was beginning to feel the effect of the screwdriver that he had drunk hastily, out of thirst, couldn't tell if it was the same room in which they had had hors d'oeuvres or some other room that had magically appeared to one side. Round tables of eight were scattered around the room, like the spokes of a wheel, focusing on a dais on which, like a king and queen, Sternbach and his bride were seated, beaming down on the assembled multitude. A loud Latin American band ripped into a few clanging specialties. Preminger and Muriel were guided to a table with a group of unidentified relatives of various sizes and ages and immediately presented with large bowls of matzo ball soup.

There was the wedding waltz. By now the bride seemed to have recovered. Her face was flushed and radiant and she swirled back and forth in her long dress like Scarlett O'Hara. Sternbach was not a good dancer—in fact, it was hard to tell from his jerky, bouncing steps if he was doing a waltz or some Greek folk dance, but he seemed to be enjoying himself hugely. He mugged and clowned, laughing in a booming voice that could be heard even above the Latin American band. Preminger silently fought his way through the matzo ball soup. He and Muriel had not spoken since the incident before the ceremony and now it seemed impossible, with all this noise, to discuss anything.

"Should we dance?" Muriel said suddenly as other couples were gathering on the floor. "What do you think?"

Preminger was not at ease on a dance floor. He knew the steps in a vague kind of way, but he always felt a sneaking urge to look at his feet and make sure they didn't perform outlandish feats. Reluctantly he said, "Sure, if you like."

They rose, luckily, just as the band was swinging into a more conventional fox trot. Preminger felt Muriel against him and rested his hand lightly on her bare back; her skin was fragrant and faintly moist with sweat. They danced seriously, not speaking, both gazing in different directions. Sternbach, who at that moment came dancing by, roared at them, "Hey, what's the matter? This isn't a funeral, folks. Buck up!" A few moments later he reappeared and tapped Preminger on the shoulder. "Mind if I—"

"No, go right ahead," Preminger said. He had expected they would be switching partners, but Sternbach appeared to have no partner at that moment. Preminger retreated silently to the table, where a harried waiter was dispensing fruit cocktail. Beside Preminger was seated a very stout woman in a flowered print dress who was eyeing a fifth of Jack Daniels that was tucked under the center display of gladiolas. "Want some?" she said to Preminger in a friendly way.

He shook his head.

She reached out and brought the bottle closer to her plate, then in a moment it had disappeared. Preminger looked down and saw that at her feet she had a large shopping bag, already half filled with napkin-wrapped goodies of different kinds. Seeing his glance, she explained hastily, "It's for my daughter, Shirley. I'm Beverly's aunt. I don't think I know you, do I? You're not Charlie Greer, are you? I didn't think so. Shirley wanted to come, but she's expecting any day now and she didn't think it would be safe, you know what I mean? So I thought I'd bring her a few souvenirs."

Shirley must have quite an appetite, Preminger thought, looking at the bag, but already he saw the woman's eyes roving over the table with predatory zeal. "Nice gladiolas," she said, smiling faintly.

"Yes, they are," Preminger said, picturing her laden down, at the end of the wedding, under a bower of fading flowers. He looked around for Muriel and Sternbach. At first they were nowhere in sight. Then, as he searched harder, he saw them off to one side. They were dancing a rumba and Muriel was moving gracefully—Preminger saw her hips swaying under the pink dress. Her face looked flushed and laughing, tendrils of hair had escaped at the nape of her neck. Were they speaking? About what? But even so, whether they were speaking or not, the expression on her face—blurred though it was by distance but seeming casual, happy, relaxed—sent a pang through him. Suddenly, as though out of nowhere, a sharp, savage sexual jealousy took possession of him. He sat glaring at the two of them, feeling almost a pain in his stomach from the intensity of his feeling. This was what it came to. All those stories about Sternbach and what a boor he was, what a slob, what a villain. Sure, but so what? Women liked that kind of thing. Muriel was no exception. And shouldn't he have grown suspicious from the very vehemence of her attacks? Methinks the lady doth protest too much. Preminger stared and stared, feeling the bitterness inside him as though it were an actual taste of something bad he had eaten. How about those Sunday afternoons when Sternbach did show up to see the boy? Was that how the custom arose of taking him over to Mother's for an hour or two to get him out of the way? Sternbach was hardly the type to give up possession of a woman just because she was no longer legally his. And Muriel—well, out of nostalgia, out of weakness, out of anything, just sexual attraction perhaps, Preminger could see her laughing, giving in, later maybe having mild regrets. Hadn't she confessed that the first time she had slept with him it had been out of an impulse, not really knowing him that well at the time? Then he had been pleased at her confessing this, as a tribute to himself, but now he saw it could as easily be reversed. If not him, then someone else. Yes, that was what galled him most of all—who was he in this whole sordid mess? Good-natured Stanley who would put up with all these shenanigans without complaining just because he was, as Mrs. Wallerstein had so kindly stated, "a sweet man." Yes, they all had him typed, all right. Probably it was expected that even if he and Muriel married, Sternbach was to be allowed to come and visit as always, to have the privileges of lord of the manor, while he was to sit genially, grinning and nodding like some Chinese Buddha.

"... be real silver?" the woman next to him was saying.

"What?" said Preminger, starting out of his gloomy reverie and tearing his eyes from Muriel and Sternbach, who were now immersed in a lively tango.

"I wonder if this is real," the woman said.

Preminger saw that she was holding a knife in one hand, holding it up to the light. He glanced warily at her bag. What next? The plates too? The legs of the table? "It doesn't look too real to me," he said.

"Sweetie, you're not dancing." It was Muriel who had found her way across to the table again. Her face was as pink as a rose from all the dancing and the edge of one bra strap was dangling loose.

Preminger said nothing. He stared at her coldly, as though she were a stranger.

She slipped in beside him. "Whew," she said, taking up a napkin and patting it to her brow. "I'm not up to all this. I'm not in shape."

"It looked like you were doing all right," he said dryly.

Something in his tone must have come across to her. She

looked at him, surprised, her eyes widening. "Why didn't *you* dance?" she said. "You could have."

"I've been having too good a time sitting here watching you."

His sarcasm nearly misfired. At first she seemed to think he was paying her a compliment, then she looked at him more closely. "What—was I overdoing it?" she said. "Did it look silly?"

"On the contrary. You looked like you were having the time of your life," Preminger said. "Why'd you stop?"

"Because I'd had enough," she said. She looked at him again and, seeing his unrelenting expression, glanced at her watch. "You know, we could leave now," she said hesitantly. "I mean, it's nearly five-thirty. I don't want Mother to get stuck with fixing Evan supper again . . . Is that okay?"

"It's fine by me," Preminger said briefly.

They got up and wedged their way through the dancing crowd to the central dais. Preminger caught a glimpse of Mrs. Gegner doing a wild watusi with a stout, balding man in a red dinner jacket. She saw him and waved and he waved back. On the dais Sternbach was seated by himself, wolfing down a plate of roasted chicken. Preminger half expected he would start tossing the bones over one shoulder when he was done.

"We really have to go," Muriel said in a quiet voice. "It's been a wonderful wedding, Abe."

"*Already* you're leaving?" He wiped his mouth and set down a chicken leg. "The fun's just beginning."

"Well, we'd love to stay, but I left Evan with Mother and—"

"Oh sure, I understand." He nodded his head and began mopping the plate with a roll. "It's swell you two could come," he said.

Preminger smiled stiffly. "Glad to have met you," he said.

"Oh, we'll meet again, I'm sure," Sternbach said heartily. As they turned to go, he called after them, "Hey, Murie, you're really in great shape, I mean it. Why don't you come around and be my first mistress, what do you say?"

Outside it was as hot and muggy as before. Preminger stood on the streetcorner, looking for a cab. He could feel the anger churning inside him and it was almost impossible to concentrate on the task at hand. When they were in the cab, he said, trying to sound calm, "Well, are you going to take him up on his offer?"

She was sitting far apart from him, staring straight ahead, a severe brooding expression on her face. "What do you mean?" she said.

"Well, I presume he was making a serious proposition," Preminger said. "Aren't you going to accept?"

He had turned to face her. She flushed. "He was joking," she said. "You could tell that."

"Very funny," Preminger said. "I suppose I don't quite appreciate his sense of humor."

Her face looked crumpled, as though she were about to cry. "Well, do you think I do?" she said.

At this something inside Preminger seemed to explode. "But you put up with it," he said. "You encourage it. Why does he act that way unless he knows you'll let him?"

She laughed mirthlessly. "Do you think he acts just according to what I want him to do? My God, if anything it's the exact opposite."

"All I know," Preminger said truculently, also staring ahead and not at her but at the solemn photo of the cab driver's license, "is that *you* chose this man and there must have been some reason for it."

"Of course there was a reason!" Her voice was high and shaking as it always became when she was upset. "I was in love with him. I don't deny that. It had an appeal for me then, all this nonsense and carrying on. You know what my family is like—everyone sitting around talking in whispers, ultra-repressed. Well, I thought he was great with his yelling and cursing and God knows what else. I thought it meant he was a free spirit and that I'd become one, too, if I married him."

Preminger was silent a moment. "Well, that may be so, but I don't see why *I* have to put up with all of this. It seems to me *I* have certain rights and feelings in this—minor as they may seem—and among them isn't being dragged along like some prize bull to be on display. Do I take *you* along to meet Shirley? Do I expose *you* to—"

"—the right corner, sir?" the cab driver was saying.

Preminger glared at him. "What?" he said sharply.

"I said, Is this the right corner?" the man repeated meekly.

"Yes, yes, this is fine." Preminger reached in his pocket and handed the man a few dollars without counting the amount.

They went up in the elevator in silence, both staring at the colored numbers as they lit up from floor to floor. As they were getting out, Preminger said with a painful smile, "It's rather clever of you to have thought of this deal with your mother."

"What deal?" She was looking at the floor and not at him.

The piteous expression on her face usually would have evoked pity in him, but at the moment it seemed to stimulate him only to want to hurt her. "To have a place to dump the kid while you and Sternbach screw away the afternoon. Very convenient."

The expression in her eyes as she stared back at him told him his remark had hit home. She looked frightened and cowed, like an animal felled by an unexpected blow.

They stood in silence, staring at Mrs. Wallerstein's door, vainly trying to compose themselves. Already Preminger felt a pang of remorse at the gratuitous cruelty of what he had said, but pride held him back from adding anything to soften it. Finally he reached out and pressed the doorbell.

Evan came running to meet them, holding up a huge sheet of paper or rather several sheets Scotch-taped together. "Hey, look," he said. "Look what we did."

They entered the apartment. Mrs. Wallerstein was in the kitchen and came out, drinking something out of a teacup. "Vodka sour," she said. "Want some? I'm recovered from the day's events."

"I'll have a beer if you have one," Preminger said.

"Look," Evan said, tugging at Preminger's sleeve and then at Muriel's. "Look! You haven't looked yet."

It was a mural of Batman and several of his henchmen, crayoned in vivid shades, with *Pow! Biff!* and *Bam!* ballooning in all directions, sprinkled with exclamation points. "Grandma helped me," Evan said. "She did all the writing."

"Yes, it's very nice," Muriel said stiffly. "Very imaginative."

Preminger took the cold beer Mrs. Wallerstein handed him and drank half of it down without speaking. He immediately felt somewhat better. He loosened his tie and draped his jacket over a chair.

"So, how was the great event?" Mrs. Wallerstein said. "Any calamities? Anyone burn themselves to death in protest?"

"It was fine," Preminger said, stretching. "A spectacle worthy of De Mille."

"So, what did you think of the great man?" she said, polishing off the rest of the vodka sour and setting the teacup down on the table. "He's a prize, isn't he? Will you give me one reason why a girl like Muriel would pick a man like that? You're a reasonable man, Prem. Give me one good reason. Here's a girl—Phi Beta Kappa, pretty—"

"Mother, will you please shut up!" Muriel said suddenly, violently. She turned on both of them. "I'm sick to death of the two of you," she said. "I'm just sick of it!" And without another word she ran, weeping, into the bathroom.

Mrs. Wallerstein looked at Preminger and shrugged her shoulders. "I put my foot in it?" she said.

"It's been a long day," Preminger said. He stood hesitantly, looking at the slammed door, then said, "I guess I—" and went slowly to open it.

He closed the door behind him. Muriel was not crying but was standing by the window, looking down into the courtyard. Preminger went over and put his hand tentatively on her shoulder, but she jerked away and said, "Everyone knows how to run my life but me! Well, it's *my* life and I can make my own mistakes. You make them, she makes them—why can't I? But at least it's a part of my past and it happened and I'm not going to pretend it didn't."

"No, I understand," Preminger said slowly. "I was a little carried away. I—"

"Do you think *I* like seeing him act the way he does?" she said, finally turning to face him, her eyes wet. "*You* hate him—can you imagine what I feel? Do you know what I'd give never to lay eyes on him again? You think he was bad today! My God, that was nothing. That was like absolutely nothing at all compared to when he gets going." She sighed and brushed back her hair. "I wanted him to see us together, to see I was happy and that he hasn't ruined my chances for being happy, even if he'd like to have. I wanted—" She stopped and her voice trailed off. "Oh, I don't know . . . I'll go wash my face."

Preminger followed her into the bathroom as she splashed water on her face and neck. The mood of intense anger was fading into a kind of erotic tenderness. He wished they were alone in the apartment. "I'm just sorry we missed a Sunday," he said.

She dried her face. "I am too," she said. "Only, listen, soon it'll be vacation. Then we can go away for a month together." She smiled, turning shyly toward him, holding the towel in one hand. "You know what I wish?" she said. "I know it sounds terrible, but sometimes—" she lowered her voice. "Sometimes I just wish we could go off—just the two of us, you know? I mean, put Evan in camp or something or leave him with Mother." As Preminger said nothing, she said, "Does that sound terrible? Am I an awful mother even to think of it?"

Preminger cleared his throat. "No, no, that doesn't sound so terrible," he said, trying to sound calm and reasonable, as though he were thinking it over. "After all, now that you mention it, he *is* old enough for camp." He went over and put his hands on her shoulders, sliding them down toward her breasts. "I don't think it sounds so terrible," he said again.

On the way home Evan ran alongside Preminger, who had Muriel's hand in his pocket, interlaced in his. "Was the wedding terrible? Grandma said it would be. She said *all* weddings are terrible."

"It depends on who's getting married," Preminger said.

THE CUCKOLD

"I said get the hell out of here and I meant it! Now scram, will you?"

Homer Congdon, standing suitcase in hand on the small country road, looked up, startled, as his host-to-be for the weekend shouted these words at full pitch into the cool night air. It was twilight, an August twilight, still not dark, and Homer saw two bent-over, harassed-looking but well-dressed people—a man and a woman—scurry down the steps of the white frame house toward a car parked in the driveway. The man who had uttered the words, Zachariah Barsotti, Homer's longtime friend, watched with what seemed satisfaction as the couple drove hastily away, first nervously knocking into a stone at one side of the road.

"Zack?" Homer said hesitantly in the ensuing quiet. Country quiet always sounded more quiet than quiet to him—he had city ears and city senses. His voice seemed unusually loud, like a stage voice prompting the main actor.

"Homer!" In one second the crumpled scowl became a wide grin. Zack bolted down the steps and flung his arm over his friend's shoulder. "Hey, here you are already! You must have made good time."

"Yes, well, the bus was a little early."

"Great! That's really great . . . Joely!" he yelled over his shoulder. "It's Homer."

A small slim figure appeared in the doorway, then darted in again. This was Zack's third wife, whom Homer had never met. He had never met wife Number One either, the infamous Suzanna, a French-speaking ceramist whom Zack had married while still a graduate student and struggling artist. Carla, Wife Number Two, Homer had known fairly well and liked—a forthright, dark-haired girl with an illegitimate baby whom Zack, in characteristic fashion, had adopted. There had been a couple of years of seeming bliss, a new baby, and then—blow up and entry of Wife Number Three, the youngest of the lot, not twenty yet, according to Zack's letter and not out of college. They kept getting younger—this was Homer's only general estimate of the situation. Of their pros and cons—why this one was prettier, that one smarter, the other one more castrating—he had only a mixed and bungled picture. He liked women now and then but did not pretend to understand them. He left that to his married friends, though none of them seemed to do a much better job of it that he could see.

"Did you see that motherfucking couple? Jesus Christ!" Zack took Homer's suitcase, carried it around a little, and set it down absently in a corner.

"Who were they?" Homer inquired.

"They came to see Zack's work," Joely said. "They thought they might buy something for the local museum." She had fair hair loose to her shoulders and a small, pinched but still pretty face, harlequin eyeglasses, and a mottled complexion. Somehow she reminded Homer of the girls photographed in shanty towns, with babies clinging to their breasts, already plummeted into an adulthood they never seem to have grasped, distracted by poverty and daydreams.

"Museum!" Zack looked disgusted. "They call that shit-

house a museum. I wish you could see the stuff they have in
that place. They stopped collecting around 1910. So now
suddenly there's this big attempt to go modern—not that any
of them know pigeon shit about any modern painter. *Or*
sculptor. Or *anything*. God, I just can't take that."

There was a pause.

"They liked some of them," Joely said timidly, looking at
no one in particular.

Zack just made a disgusted face.

Homer cleared his throat. He felt hot and sticky, his coat
clinging to his back like an unwelcome second skin.
"Well . . ." he said.

"I have these new things," Zack said quickly. "They're out
back. We'll look at them tomorrow."

"I'd like that," Homer said.

"Listen, take off your coat," Zack said, tugging at Homer's
sleeve. "*Relax*. You must be bushed. Want a beer or something?"

"We have iced tea, too," Joely said eagerly. "Or coffee. I
could make iced coffee."

"Beer's fine," Homer said.

He had thought that this first night he and Zack might
stay up talking, but half an hour later, after the beer, an
enormous, irresistible sleepiness came over him. His eyes lit-
erally seemed to drag shut. He was steered to a guest room
upstairs. "It's near the baby," Joely said. "I hope he doesn't
wake you. He's up kind of early sometimes."

That's right—there was a new baby. Zack always had
babies. How many did he have now? Homer couldn't quite
keep them straight. Babies tended to blend in his mind. But,
why not? Paternity was a profession, in its way. He was asleep
before he could pursue the thought.

In the morning there was the baby and there were
the birds. To Homer the two sounds, equally unfamiliar, be-

came a cacaphony of shrieks, like a modern symphony heard for the first time. In the background, more muffled, were sounds of padding feet, doors shutting, He tried burying his head under the pillow, but a bright summer light pierced through the tattered shades. Awakening was forced upon him.

Shaved, showered, he dawdled his way downstairs at eight. The living room was deserted, by day a jumble of old furniture, childrens' toys, a large mesh playpen squashed near the record cabinet. In the kitchen Joely was sitting in a rocker nursing the baby. No Zack. Homer smiled uneasily. "Hi."

"Oh, hi." She seemed not the least discomfited. "Gee, you're up. I thought you'd sleep ages. Zack always does weekends . . . Was it the baby?"

"Oh, no, babies—he—"

"Yeah, it's a boy. It's hard to tell at this age." She smiled and with deft economy transferred the baby to the opposite breast, covering the other loosely with a cloth. Her breasts were large and blue-veined but, still, it was a maternal scene, not a seductive one. Should he look at them? At her? He tried looking at her face, but the breasts were so close to it, it was hard to avoid appearing to gaze their way.

"Listen, take some juice. It's right in there," she said. "Sorry I can't—"

Homer helped himself to juice.

Joely rocked, the baby sucked. "So, you're—what? Something with stocks?"

"I deal in arbitrage, mainly," Homer said.

"You're not married or anything, I guess," she offered.

The remark seemed ingenuous. Homer shook his head. About this he felt not really uncomfortable. Most of his friends knew his sexual proclivities, accepted them if they didn't share them. He wasn't ostentatious, had no desire to convert, rather regarded his inclination as a thing that had "turned out that way"—that suited him. And at times, rarely, he'd even thought of marriage in spite of it, to a cultivated, wealthy woman with interests of her own, say. But none such had ventured his way and he wasn't itching for it.

"It must be funny, not being married," Joely went on.

"Not funny, really," Homer said. He'd gotten to like the way she spilled things out, seemingly without forethought.

"No, it's just—well, I guess I've always lived with *someone.* I'm one of seven, you know. Did Zack mention that? So, like, I've always been around *people* . . . I think I'd feel sort of lonely living all by myself."

"No, there is that," Homer said. "That's true."

"Of course, men are different," she added quickly, as though afraid of having hurt his feelings.

He smiled.

"Does this bother you?" she said. "I mean, I could do it in another room. Some men—"

"It's fine," he said. Though he did wonder when Zack would appear.

"Zack's talked about your visit so much," she said, rocking, bemused.

"I wanted to come sooner."

She seemed not to have heard this, in any case went on, oblivious. "He's been kind of—Zack's been kind of—well, it's been a hard year for him."

"The divorce—"

"Oh, that—well, no. But—this year. It's funny, like all these years he looked forward to just having time off, just to sculpt, but I think it gets on his nerves, kind of. He needs something to *do.*" She lowered her voice. "But, listen, don't tell him I said that. I mean, it may not even be true. *I* don't know . . . But I think he was happier before."

"He's a very energetic man," Homer said.

"That's it! He is!" Relief made her lean forward and the breasts seemed to jump out at him. "And now—well, it's just too much free time." The baby's head rolled to one side; he let the large brown nipple pop from his mouth. "Drunken sailor, huh? They don't know when they have it good." Detached from its object, the baby's mouth continued to move in small kissing motions. Homer watched it with a kind of repelled fascination, like watching a deepsea fish in an aquarium behind glass. "Want to hold him a second? I'll put on coffee." Without an assent, the baby was his. He sat stiffly, holding the round, blanket-clad object as though it were a bomb that might, at any moment, explode.

"You don't like them. Come on, out with it!" Zack said.

"I didn't *say* that," said Homer.

Zack snorted. "Christ, Homer, will you—"

"I'm trying to decide," Homer said quickly. He stepped back and stared carefully at the large metal object rising nearly to the roof of the reconverted shed Zack used as a studio. The statue was made of fenders molded together and painted in deliberately garish colors, the total effect being a kind of grotesque modern totem pole. Zack had made his career on fenders. When Homer had first known him, he was turning out small, beautifully wrought granite pieces of animals, nudes, seated thinkers. Then one day Carla, coming upon a fender in a dusty road somewhere—so the by now apocryphal tale went—had taken it home, kept it around until Zack, more out of curiosity, had tried to see what he could do with it. From then on he was made. Fenders opened the road to everywhere—one man shows, museums, teaching appointments. And even now with Carla out of the way, the fender remained, its part in Zack's life evidently not subject to the same whims as those of passion and married life.

"It's an interesting idea, using the color," Homer said carefully, "but somehow before—"

"It's a mistake," Zack said curtly.

"What?"

"Showing these things to people. I don't know what's wrong with me. It's stupid. It's always been this way. You ask this one, that one—that's stupid! What difference does it make! You should just go do it."

"Yeah, well, there's something in that," Homer said. "I just thought—"

"I mean, what do *you* know?" Zack said. "What does it all mean to you?"

Homer was silent. He was used to Zack's turns of mood, rages, depressions; nonetheless, after an absence they always disconcerted him. Zack's spiky red hair stood on end. He looked both handsome and somewhat menacing, not just playing at it.

The dog, a large collie, ambled into the room. Zack seized it by the fur and began stroking it. "So, what's new in commodities?" he said.

"Nothing much," Homer said.

"Just watching the dollars pile up."

"Sure."

Irony, but still this was his role evidently—the financially secure bachelor, untroubled by the vagaries of art, passion, et al.

"How do you like Joely?" Zack said suddenly, still pulling at the dog's tawny fur.

"Oh, I—I like her," Homer said. "She seems very . . . spontaneous."

Zack laughed. "Yeah, she's that . . . Didn't bother you, her nursing like that in front of you?"

"Oh no, not at all."

"Not that her figure's so great. I mean, Carla used to do that and every friend I had would end up getting a hard on. Whereas Joely, I don't know. She doesn't move them around the same way."

"How *is* Carla?" Homer asked. He glanced once more at the totem pole. To the side was a pile of welding tools, arranged on a wooden bench.

"Fine, jes' fine," Zack said. "I mean, she's out of that hospital. I guess she's on her feet again."

Carla, despite her seeming resilience and toughness, had been having breakdowns since the age of fourteen. Homer had sometimes felt her neurosis provided too much competition for Zack's, being, when given full rein, more colorful and dramatic, with a certain feminine intricacy and irrationality.

"I always liked Carla," Homer said thoughtfully, picking up a metal tool and scraping at the wooden bench.

"Yeah, she liked you, too . . . She always asks after you. I guess she would've seduced you, if she could."

Homer smiled. "She should've tried."

Zack looked at him with a peculiar expression.

They were silent.

Zack remained in a bad mood. At badminton—they had a few rounds after lunch—he was sullen and disagreeable, deliberately missing shots, cheating, getting angry. Homer was no athlete, but just by keeping his cool, he beat Zack in eight games out of ten, finally suggested quitting because the atmosphere was so bad. Look, I'm a guest, he told himself, relaxing in the hammock with a lemonade afterward. The hell with this shit. Let him behave.

But Zack continued to sulk like a spoiled child. He shouldn't show his stuff, then, if he's so hypersensitive, Homer thought, washing for dinner. I didn't ask to see them. Who came all this way just for old time's sake, just to be friendly?

Dinner—steaks broiled out of doors, eaten on the screened-in porch—was a tête-à-tête, mainly Joely's ambling, uncertain monologue, interspersed with "interested" questions by Homer. Zack, hunched over his food, ate ravenously and silently, then disappeared while they were having coffee.

They were, it appeared, going to a party. In silence all three piled into Zack's old Volvo and were off. Joely had changed. But in her black cotton dress, a large modern pin affixed to her shoulder, some vague attempt at makeup, she looked to Homer's eyes only younger, like a high school girl going to a dance in the school gym, wearing her older sister's hand-me-downs. Zack, in the same checked shirt and jeans he'd been wearing since Homer's arrival, drove fast, letting the car bump its way over rocks or whatever was in its path.

At a large split level house—smoke, drinks. Homer, disconsolate, annoyed, wandered around a spacious unfurnished living room and stared at the paintings on the wall. Evidently the vision he'd had of long intimate discussions between himself and Zack about art and life was a pipe dream. Why the invitation, then? Why bother coming? He drank vodka, ate peanuts, and scowled.

Zack appeared to be having a great time. It even seemed—this Homer caught from snatches of overheard conversation—that the party was in Zack's honor. Upon their arrival a swoop of women descended upon him. Joely and Homer were unceremoniously cast aside in the shuffle. As the party wore on, Homer caught glances of Zack talking volubly, laughing loudly, pressed up against a woman in red with orange hair. Envy descended, coloring the irritation. It was or had always been like this. Something about Zack, wherever he went, provoked anger, love, hostility, sympathy—strong feelings, in any case. An encounter in a lunchroom could lead to an undying friendship or a lifelong feud—over whether or not to order banana cream pie. Whereas Homer, even when he tried—and he rarely had the courage—could not, for the life of him, inspire these intenser passions. When he worked himself up to a scene, no one knew it had been one except himself, even when it was over. He would have liked to scream and rant, but clearly it wasn't his calling. He was liked usually—that was all, just *liked*. In this stuffy room it seemed a deathlike fate.

"Gosh, it's *hot* in here, isn't it?" Joely appeared, hair disheveled, upper lip perspiring. She looked around brightly. "They're so excited—this statue Zack said he'd do for the library. At first all these founding fathers and types like that got all livid. They thought it was obscene. Then they loved it!" She laughed, a little drunkenly.

A man in tight purple pants and a ruffled white shirt drifted by. "Oh, there's—do you know him?" Joely said. "He's—oh dear, he's going away. He's this very interesting man. Zack knows him. Fergus Stone—I wish I'd—you'd like him . . . maybe. I mean—"

In her fluttering he detected, more than anything, a wish to be nice, so if he tried he might avoid the implied insult. Was he, to her inner eye, a wearer of purple pants? He could have been angry if it hadn't seemed so ingenuous.

"Where's Zack?" she said a few moments later, as Homer was pouring more warm vodka into a paper cup and wondering what to do with it.

"I don't *know*. Isn't he around? I thought I saw him."

"I can't *find* him," she said anxiously. "I mean, like, he just isn't *here*."

"Oh, he must be *somewhere*," Homer assured her. Together, like two children lost at the beach, they wandered about the jovial, inebriated guests, questioning, "Have you seen . . ." "Is Zack . . .?" After a half hour it appeared he just wasn't there. Someone said he'd driven off.

Joely stared at Homer. "But he has the *car*," she said.

Homer frowned. "Maybe he'll come back."

"I don't care! I want to go *home*." She seemed tearful and easily collapsible, perhaps with drink. He felt unsteady himself. "He told someone he was going home."

Might he be off screwing someone, the woman in red, under some bushes? This seemed a likely denouement, but, turning, Homer saw the woman in red seated in a basket chair talking to a portly man in a black turtleneck. Another woman in red perhaps?

They ended up walking home. It wasn't far, Joely said. She wanted air, she said. Homer, discreetly, nervously, as though this were his wife, agreed. They were quiet, walking. Even Joely seemed to be stilled by the soft expanse of silent night around them.

"He'd been in this funny mood—I told you," she said as they were within view of the house.

"He does this often?"

"Oh no! Never!"

On this note of confusion they reached home. No Zack. No car.

For two hours they sat in the dark, waiting for him, Joely leaning against a tree, Homer swinging in the hammock, gazing, vodka-bemused, at stars. Some seemed to be shooting, but he wasn't sure.

"So, how'd it go?" Zack, smiling, appeared behind Homer just as he was plugging in his electric shaver.

They'd given up waiting for him the night before and had gone off to their individual beds. Had he just returned? It was eight A.M. "How did *what* go?" Homer said.

"It . . . You know . . . What's the matter, didn't I give you time enough?"

Homer looked at him curiously. "Where were *you?*" he said.

"Me? I just cleared off. Figured you two ought to be alone together."

"Joely and—"

"Yeah, Joely and you. Thought you'd have a lot to talk over."

"About what?"

"Things."

Homer stood, shaver in hand, uneasy. "I don't know exactly what you're getting at, Zack."

Zack just smiled. "Oh, cut it, Homer. Listen, I don't care. I told you. It's okay with me. If she wants it, let her. You too. Always oblige a friend, you know."

There was a crash from the bedroom as though something had been dropped. Zack turned. "Guess she's getting up . . . Why don't you go in? You can do it again. I'll go fix some breakfast." With this he turned and began to amble down the stairs.

"Zack, listen—" Homer began.

"Go and get her!" Zack yelled. His pupils were like cracked marbles—green, brown.

"I don't *want* to," Homer said suddenly, angrily.

"You don't want to? Why not?"

"I don't even know what you're talking about," he stumbled. Had he made a mistake? Was it a joke? Feigned madness as a gag?

"Isn't she as good as Suzanna?"

"Suzanna? . . . I never *knew* Suzanna."

"Never knew her? Sure you did."

"No, I never—I never even *met* Suzanna."

Zack looked at him curiously. "Is that right?"

"Sure." Homer tried smiling. "You remember. We met after you got divorced from—"

Zack smiled. "That's right. So we did. It was—Carla. Yeah, that's it."

Homer's eyes widened; his heart was beating as though he'd been running from something. "What *about* Carla?" he said.

"She told me all about you two. Listen, I'm telling you, I don't mind. I mean it. You can't believe that, can you? I know all the stuff that went on. She told me. She told me everything."

"Zack, there's some mistake. Carla and I never—"

"She told me all the details, man. I can tell you where, I can tell you how, I know it all."

Joely, in a pink housedress, emerged from the bedroom, her hair in curlers. "Hi, Homer!" she said. She just looked at Zack.

"Honey, Homer just won't believe I don't care about you and him. Tell him I don't care."

"Don't care what?" Her voice had a morning hoarseness. She squinted as though the light were too bright.

"Did I ever mind when you did it with anyone else? You know I didn't. I'm not a stingy man. Share the wealth! That's the Barsotti motto. Spread it around!"

It went on like that all morning. Homer finally locked himself in his room, packed faster than he ever had in his life, and was out the door in no time. He was worried for Joely's sake, but cowardice got the upper hand. Violence in the city was recognizable, anyway. He headed for hot, tense Manhattan with relief.

Later he heard through friends that Zack was committed to a local institution, then released a few months later. No one seemed all that surprised. Thinking about it, Homer thought he shouldn't have been either. Joely he ran into one Saturday afternoon in New York. She was standing in front of FAO Schwarz, gazing at a life-size giraffe.

"Oh, he's fine now," she told Homer. "He's on these— some kind of drug, I forget the name. *Per* something. It's helped him so *much*. He's a different person."

"I'm glad," Homer said, meaning it.

"It really all started with Carla. He had this thing about her being unfaithful. I don't know why. I mean, was she?"

"Not that I know of," Homer said. "I'm meeting her for a drink later. Would you like to come?"

"Oh, I'd love that."

And so it was that at five that afternoon he found himself ensconced at the Plaza, an attractive woman on either flank, the three of them imbibing merrily. The women had eyes only for each other. Their talk, starting in generalities, soon dissolved into an orgy of gossip and shared trivia. But in the eyes of a poet, a friend of Zack's, who entered and saw them together, Homer saw that for once in his life he was considered the center of a scandal—not superfluous. It tasted more intoxicating than his third martini.

SLEEPING PILLS

"Before I forget, here are the pills," Isidor said, reaching into his pocket. He placed a small plastic container of red capsules on the coffee table. Perhaps, he thought, he should have handed them to her directly. What had held him back was his uncertainty that he was acting properly in giving them to her at all. Not that he believed her to be on the verge of suicide, but he knew she was unhappy. For the hour he had sat there, drinking iced tea with her, he had felt divided between wanting to help her and trying to assure himself that neither her life nor what she did with it was his responsibility.

"Thank you," Rebecca said, but she did not take the bottle. She just sat looking at it, as a child might look at an expensive present brought by a friend of her parents. She saw his hesitation—he was never good at concealing what he felt—and it touched her that he should be concerned about her. "You needn't worry about it," she said, smiling at him wryly. "I won't betray you by doing anything foolish."

"Oh, of course not," he reassured her hastily. "Don't be silly . . . You like that type? They're the right strength, and so on?" A month and a half ago he had brought her another similar bottle of sleeping pills. He received all drugs from his brother-in-law who was a chemist and was in general accustomed to dispensing them to friends. But he felt that his reassurance was for her sake and did not quite ring true. He had been surprised that she had asked for more so soon after the other request, having expected the others would last her for several months.

"I have been unhappy," she acknowledged, putting aside his reassurance and turning to what was really on his mind. "And I do sleep badly, but I don't think—I really don't—that I'm a suicidal sort of person. I mean, some people are and others aren't. And I've always felt that ultimately I wasn't, even though the thought might cross my mind at certain moments." She looked up at him, and as always, his eyes, dark and shadowy behind his glasses, seemed to reflect understanding and concern. "For one thing," she went on, warmed by this expression, "my career has been doing well since the divorce, so it does give me something to turn to. And I'm glad of that."

Isidor nodded. He reached out and touched the bottle of pills with one finger. "How did that screen test go?" he said. "I meant to ask you." Even about this he felt slightly guilty. There had been a time when he followed her career very closely, made a point of trying to see the shows in which she appeared—usually off-Broadway things that didn't run very long—but lately he had been concerned with his own affairs, and although she had told him a few weeks ago that she would be on TV, he had forgotten to watch the program.

Rebecca kept her eyes focused on his hand as it touched the bottle of pills. "It went well, in a sense," she said. "That is, I didn't get the part, so you could say ultimately it didn't go well. But they said they liked the screen test very much. They even told me at one point that I had the part. I got terribly excited and went out and spent a lot of the money and then they said they'd decided they couldn't afford to cast an unknown. That had been the whole point, that they *had* wanted an unknown. But I guess they got cold feet. It's understandable; they've put so much money into it. They picked Sally Field in the end." She had been sure that Isidor would somehow disapprove if she had gotten the part. There were good people connected with the movie, the script was by a well-known writer, but basically it was a commercial effort of the kind he had always fulminated against when he had written a column on the theater. There was no need for her even to conjure up the complete irony with which he would have regarded "her" part, a kind of backwoods Lolita type who went around throughout most of the movie clad in deerskin breeches, darting in and out of pine forests like a parody of Rima the Bird Girl.

"It's too bad from the point of view of the money," Isidor said. "I suppose you could use some now." He had never been certain and had never asked how much alimony she was receiving from her former husband. Doubtless it was not much or, at any rate, did not come regularly. Why had she picked such a man for a husband? Arrogant, unpleasant, good-looking, vain—the kind of man he could understand her having been attracted to but not marrying. He had disliked him from the first evening they had met. At that time he had not seen Rebecca for over two years. She had been out on the Coast with some repertory company and there she had met Tadek, a Hungarian refugee who had pretenses of wanting to be a producer, though he lacked, to Isidor's mind, both the financial and the professional qualifications. He had expressed nothing of his feelings then, particularly since he saw Tadek looking at him with jealous eyes, as though trying to size him up: Former lover? Former friend? He never knew how much she had told him of their earlier relationship.

"Actually, right now money isn't a problem," Rebecca said. "I mean, of course, it always is, living in New York, but in fact I've felt as though I were living rather luxuriously this year. That place I had with Tadek was so terribly dark and dreary it used to depress me just to come home. Whereas here there's so much light, the ceilings are so high, it's really very cheerful and nice."

She hoped she was not sounding too Pollyannaish. Ever since her divorce, when she had begun seeing Isidor again for occasional lunches and dinners, she had felt as though she must tread a thin line with him. She had heard it said of divorced women—and she felt it was true of herself—that they had a kind of desperate air, wanting sympathy, attention, especially from men. And she knew that he would be ready to give it if she showed the slightest need. But she wanted to spare him that, spare him and herself as well. It seemed to her it would be degrading their friendship, which for so many years had meant a great deal to her.

"Yes, I remember I used to wonder why you stayed in that place," Isidor said, smiling. "It did seem a kind of hellhole. Susan used to say—" He stopped midway.

"Say what?" questioned Rebecca.

"Say you must feel uncomfortable there, after your parents' home," Isidor said, amending his wife's comment. Usually he made a strict point of not mentioning Susan to Rebecca, although the two women did not get along that badly. On Rebecca's part he felt there was basically indifference; his wife was not the kind of woman with whom she would be friends. Most of her women friends seemed to belong to the theatrical world: dancers, actresses, singers. On his wife's part there was a kind of envy that had been submerged into admiration and, at times, malice. Long ago, when they were just married, he and Susan had visited Rebecca at her parents' home. They had both felt uncomfortable in the huge Park Avenue apartment with its giant, air-cooled lobby lined with walls of smoked glass, obsequious doormen and elevator men popping out from corners, pressing buttons, whispering thank yous. At that time Susan's attitude had been simple: envy of all this conspicuous consumption. He had felt a touch of this, but mainly he had felt the visit had given him an insight into Rebecca, her rebelliousness, her fierce contempt for personal possessions, her outlandish way of dressing. Although she had bright red hair, she always wore dresses of lavender, pink, and scarlet. At one point in the evening her father, a stout, aggressive Jewish businessman, a more successful version of his own father, had taken him aside and whispered, "You've known her a long time. What does she want, huh? Can you tell me that? I'd give her anything—minks, a car—just let her ask me. What more does she want?" He had never told Rebecca about the incident.

"Is Susan well?" Rebecca asked. "You had said she was feeling down at the mouth over losing that job. Did she get another?" She tried, when she spoke of Susan, to bend over backward to be fair, but at heart she felt, as she always had, that Susan was not worthy of Isidor. She was a step up from his first wife, that was true, for Dora had been a kind of ninny with her big flowered hats and bleached blond hair and simpering manner—exactly the kind of small-town Protestant that a Jewish man wanting to break away from his family would marry. Yes, certainly Susan was more intelligent and even more attractive, but there was something so literal-minded about her, Rebecca thought, so earnest and dogmatic, always concerned with causes and picketing. Not that one ought not to be concerned—and being married to Isidor perhaps one would become so inevitably—but why not do it with some sense of style and humor? Or wasn't that possible?

"Yes, she has a new job," Isidor said. "She's working at a school for mentally disturbed children."

"And she likes it?" Rebecca asked.

"Quite a lot, yes." Isidor had resolved not to complain about Susan to Rebecca. It was quite simply that he disliked that kind of man, the kind who was always moaning and groaning about his wife to other women, railing about being misunderstood. For the last six months it had seemed to him that there was a good possibility he would separate from Susan. Then lately he had swung back, feeling that at forty-three he was not ready for all the fuss and bother of a divorce, for the new start on life. He'd had enough of that, he felt. It was different for Rebecca at thirty-five; she could afford to be optimistic about the future, He didn't want to discourage her just on the basis of his own failures, which undoubtedly were as much his fault as anyone else's.

"Will you leave the city, now that you have this fellowship?" Rebecca said. "Go to Europe or something?" As she said this, she found herself hoping, for the first time, that he would not go. And again she reminded herself that his life was not her affair, one way or the other. She looked at him a moment since just then he was staring, bemused, out of the window. It seemed to her he had become more attractive than when she had first known him twelve years ago. At that time he had been just a beginning director at a small drama school where she was attending classes. They were presenting a Japanese Noh play and after class he used to gather the actors together and lecture them on the background of the play, its history and religious meaning. They were all very absorbed in it, Rebecca remembered, and even took exercise classes in Zen where, with utter intensity, they spent hours trying to "feel" the back of their necks. When he lectured, Isidor had sat on the edge of the stage with the actors scattered around the auditorium, listening to him. Most of the actors sat in the middle or the back—Rebecca herself had sat way off to one side in the fifth row—but one girl always sat in the first row in the very center. She was a very beautiful Japanese girl with a long coil of black hair that hung down her back like a snake and a sinuous, liquid way of moving, as though she were an elegant fish. This girl was having a love affair with Isidor, a fact that was not common knowledge,

though his unhappy marriage was. He had a habit of address-
ing all his remarks directly to this girl, as though everything
he said, no matter how esoteric or abstract, was part of some
intense, profound dialogue between the two of them. This
had irritated Rebecca, though at the same time she found
herself watching him with curiosity and even fascination, trying to understand how one man could have married such a
vapid idiot—none of the actors had liked Dora, who often
came backstage with her two children—and then chosen as a
mistress such a strange, exotic girl. It was, Rebecca had
thought, like a man who habitually dined on steak and pota-
toes suddenly showing a taste for seaweed soup or eels au
gratin. For some reason this girl chose her as a confidante and
used to reveal, in an almost compulsive way, every detail of
her affair. Thus, long before she knew Isidor in more than a
casual, professional way, she had known the most intimate
details of his emotional and sexual life, a fact that at first had
made her distinctly uneasy in his presence. But at that time,
perhaps because of the confidences of the Japanese girl, she
had not found him attractive. He had seemed to her to be
brash and headstrong, always giving a kind of bravura per-
formance while directing, trying to tell all the actors how to
interpret their parts. Now, perhaps due to success or just to
the wearing down process of life, he seemed calmer, more
reflective. Even his face, lined now around the eyes and
mouth, as though a cat had made fine, quick scratches with
its claws, had an appeal for her that it had not had then.

"I may go to Italy," Isidor said, turning from the window.
"I would like to go to Germany, too, just to see some of the
things they're doing. Certainly if I do that Brecht next year,
I'd like to have an idea of how they're handling it. But we'll
see. I haven't decided definitely."

As he spoke he was aware of her looking at him. He found
her more beautiful than she had seemed to him when he had
met her throughout the year for lunch or dinner. At those

times she was always all dressed up, about to meet her agent or appear at an audition. She would be wearing some elegant, fashionable outfit, would be made up to the hilt in heavy eye makeup, her hair elaborately arranged. Now, in her slacks and man's shirt, with her hair loose, her face bare of adornment, she reminded him more of the way she had looked years ago, as a drama student. The other way she looked like the kind of woman men would turn to watch in a public restaurant—as, in fact, he had seen them doing—but he preferred this simpler way. "How about you?" he said. "Since that film thing didn't materialize, where do you go from there?"

Rebecca sighed. "The perennial question," she said. "I don't know. They did say because they liked the test, they would be interested in doing some TV series. And the thing is, it would pay well. They said in a year I'd have half a million dollars."

Isidor raised his eyebrows and whistled.

"Yes—no, I know, it's a lot of money—but it's a trap, too. If you accept it, you can't do anything else. You're stuck with them for five years. And who ever hears of a TV actress? Except mass America. But who wants that? It's typical. I sat around, pretending to think over the offer, writing down all these lists of why I should and why I shouldn't accept. But I knew all along that in the end I'd turn it down. You just have to."

Just as she was in the midst of talking, something entered her head. "TV actress" had been what reminded her. It was that she had seen someone recently who had said Isidor was leaving his wife for a TV actress, someone fairly well known but no one she would have expected him to marry. She was used to hearing about Isidor's affairs from one person or another and, while never indifferent to the news, always took it with a grain of salt and tried to minimize whatever jealousy she felt at the time. But to marry a TV actress! It seemed so undignified, somehow. She would have liked to ask him about it now but forced herself not to. After all, she did not confide in him about her personal life. Why should he confide in her?

"I think you were right to turn it down," Isidor said. "I mean, the hell with money. Who needs it?"

Rebecca laughed.

"I'm serious. You need enough to live on, to live comfortably, but you have that. What do you need with half a million dollars?"

She had heard about Eva; he sensed that from her face as she was talking about making money on TV. Since they had never discussed it, he saw no reason to inform her that it was a thing of the past and had been for over a month. Yet he would have liked to mention it, if only because he did regard it as, in some sense, a lapse of taste on his part. He had what he regarded as an unfortunate attraction to a certain kind of all-American, freckled, blond girl or woman, such as Dora had been when he first met her. But it was a taste he could not accept in any rational or intellectual way; he had tried to get away from it by marrying Susan, who was as dark and Jewish as Dora had been fair and Protestant.

"No, I don't need the money," Rebecca said. "Or, at least, that's the least of what I need at the moment." As she said this, she wished right away that she could retract it. She felt certain he would fill in the accurate answer: What you need is a man. Was she getting hypersensitive about this subject? Or was it Isidor's presence that made her so? It was all very well for him. He had always seemed to manage all these fairly intricate relationships with women and still go on working, leading a reasonably normal life, but with her love affairs always seemed to lead to some total upset, some fundamental rearrangement. Not that there was anything wrong with upsets in themselves, but at times, times like now, she felt that stability, order, calmness, were what she most wanted, or at any rate—it was evidently not quite the same thing—what she most ought to want.

"Did you like that sculptor the Willises dug up for you?" Isidor said. Recently he had been at a party given by a couple, the Willises, whom he and Susan had seen socially for many years. Rebecca had known Arthur Willis, who was a producer, from a revival in which she had once appeared. He knew that Willis was interested in Rebecca and had seen her a few times for lunch. He was not jealous; Willis was not exactly a romantic figure, being stout and bald, though he was powerful in the world of the theater and had that aura of dynamism that derived from such power. But he had felt jealous of the man the Willises had invited for her, a sculptor of about thirty-five, strikingly handsome, with a foreign accent of some kind. He was sure the man would remind her of her former husband, and although this resemblance might have made her wary, it had seemed to him she was interested. He had watched as they left together and had seen the man, as he slipped the coat over her shoulders, run his hand halfway down her back; she was wearing one of those backless summer dresses. For the rest of the evening he had been in a bad mood.

"No, I didn't like him especially," Rebecca said. "He seemed worn out, somehow, as though he'd had too many affairs, too much of everything, I felt." She did not feel like adding that she found him physically attractive; it could become chronic, like a disease. She did regard that evening as a triumph of will, however, since she had not allowed the man in for a drink, feeling, correctly she felt later, that she could not trust herself with him alone. And why had she thought she could trust herself with Isidor alone? Probably that had been a mistake, too. Why not have arranged to meet him at a restaurant or in some impersonal place? There was no need to be testing herself continually. She had done well enough in this last year, well in the sense that her life had been the very image of respectability, not well only in the toll it had taken on her—the insomnia, for one thing. "Did you ever have insomnia, Isidor?" she asked suddenly.

He hesitated a moment before answering. "Once, yes. There was a time about ten years ago when I had it rather badly. It was that time right after I'd left Dora."

"How did you cure it, or did it just go away by itself?" Rebecca asked.

Again Isidor hesitated before saying, "I went to a psychiatrist for a while . . . And that seemed to help. At least I haven't had it since." He had been reluctant to mention the psychiatrist to her simply because he felt she would look upon it ironically. She had always had a theory that life should be lived with style and elegance, and undoubtedly psychiatry seemed to her too stuffy and scientific a way of approaching personal problems. He himself had shared this attitude to an extent but during the therapy had gradually given it up.

"I've thought of going on and off during this year," Rebecca said, "but I never could work up the courage or whatever. And then I suppose I keep thinking I have enough realistic problems to handle, without dealing with unconscious ones and all that. Plus, the money thing, of course."

Yet it confounded all her impressions of Isidor that he had been to a psychiatrist. She had always felt that the success with which he wove his way through the tangles of his life came from not examining with overscrupulosity the motivations for his emotions; he left, she had thought, intellect for his work. But then she always tended to idealize men—that was part of her trouble—to think that simply because they were men they lacked either faults or weaknesses, and this even when logic and experience proved to the contrary. This sudden admission of weakness on Isidor's part touched her. He too might, after all, have taken sleeping pills then, so she need not be ashamed of accepting them from him. He seemed at that moment closer and more human, as he would have if he had suddenly revealed a tendency to alcoholism or an abnormal fear of heights.

"Is your insomnia bad?" Isidor said. The pills were still where he had placed them, in the center of the table. It was not just that he wanted to change the subject from his own problems; it was that he really wanted to know truthfully about her life now. All the times he had met her over the year she had seemed to him to put on a kind of front: gay, talkative, not really letting him see through to what she was thinking or feeling. He understood what could cause that feeling—he had felt the same way himself just after his own divorce—but now he felt it as a screen between them that he wanted to push aside.

"It's off and on. Sometimes bad, sometimes all right," Rebecca said cautiously. Don't be sympathetic, Isidor, she thought. She could resist anything but sympathy. Already, just at those words of his, she felt a trembling inside, a warning sign that she might give way. She did not want to weep in front of him. So far they had been successful in steering the conversation clear of what to her was the ultimate problem of her life: her loneliness, her need for another human being.

"Why don't you call me sometime when you have it," said Isidor. "It might help to talk to someone." He saw at once that her face and manner had, in fact, changed with his last remark. He did not want to hurt her; he felt already he had gone too far, but he could not resist continuing on the basis of this advantage.

"I'd wake up Susan," Rebecca said, not trusting herself to look up at him. "It wouldn't be right, anyway."

"She never wakes up at night," Isidor said. "I can turn the phone down." He knew then why he had made a point of asking to meet her at her home rather than in a restaurant. Yet still he hesitated, for a moment said nothing, then reached out and put his hands on her shoulders. "I thought I was your best friend in the city," he said. "Why shouldn't you be able to call me if you like, if it would be a help?"

At that Rebecca felt herself give way. Her whole body seemed to collapse, as though the deep feeling of loneliness had abruptly been forced to the surface, like a vein of ore crushed forward in an earthquake. She wept, pressing her face against his shoulder. I didn't want to do this, she thought. I swore I wouldn't. In the midst of her weeping there rose up in her mind Tadek's yelling out to her at the culmination of their final quarrel. "I know what you're going to do," he had said. "You're going to go off and have an affair with Isidor Seltz."

Isidor pulled her closer to him, without speaking. He stroked her head with his free hand. He felt his heart beating rapidly and his throat was dry. "Don't say anything," he said. "Don't try."

For a little while she took his advice, just letting herself give way to the luxury of tears, but finally she said, "This won't work, Isidor. How can it? It will mean that in six months we'll never see each other again."

He knew she was right, but fighting against his knowledge was a sense of hope, so that the two feelings remained in combat, like two soldiers with knives at each other's throats. "Don't try to predict the future," he said; it seemed to him this was the best and only consolation he could give her.

THE WRONG MAN

"How do you like it?"

"Great."

"No—*seriously.*"

Max Robish veered around in his office desk chair to stare at his fourteen-year-old stepdaughter, Mandy, who framed the doorway, the miniskirt, or whatever it was, revealing two freckled lengths of preadolescent flab.

"Really want to know?" he said.

Her face became uncertain. She giggled. "Not if it's something *mean.*"

He raised one eyebrow.

She blushed, hesitated. "Everyone wears them that short," she said.

"I know."

One leg was wound, storklike, around the other. "Well . . . I just thought I'd ask you."

"Sure, Mandy, any time." He veered back to regard once again the stack of pre-Christmas exams piled to one side of the desk. *The reign of Charles I was marked by civil disorder. Could you discuss in three hundred words or less the causes of this unrest?* High school history was so beautifully simple-minded. He had often had cause, in his usual deprecatory reflections on his profession, to observe this. Cause and then effect. It was lovely. He glanced at one paper. A pity about Mandy. He had often thought that the one thing that would lend a certain color to his marriage would be an intense, incestuous affair with his stepdaughter. The slyness, the mystery, the tears on all sides! But she was such a plump, dowdy little thing. Either her pubescence was being delayed or, more likely, it would never arrive. Yet sadly (for her) his sarcastic jibes that he tried, to some extent, to keep under wraps, served only to stimulate her puppyish adoration of him. If only she'd lose weight! Maybe there was a tender little body under there, God knew . . . But who cared, really? In ten years, maybe, he'd be ready for Lolitas, at fifty or sixty. Now they still reminded him uncomfortably of his own three sisters in their long-gone girlhoods, with their twisted pigtails and rubber-banded teeth—hardly an erotic vision.

He looked at the desk calendar in which a black card indicating the date had been placed. His wife did this, straightening up his things, though he had warned her off a couple of times. But if it gave her pleasure . . . Which little enough did. December 21. He had had a vague premonitory anxiety all morning, and now, staring at the date, he realized it had not been, as he had thought, the usual nausea at the arrival of the Christmas season and its related festivities. No, one year ago today Alice, his first, wife, had committed suicide. They had been divorced five years already, though he still, sporadically, kept in touch with her. She had shown no special desire to see Timmy, to whom he had been awarded custody and who was, in any case, away most of the year at camp or boarding school. She was drunk a good deal of the time, not, as in the beginning, loudly and abusively so, but almost pleasant, vague, nostalgic, incoherent. He dreaded her sober a good deal more. Already, then, she had reminded him of her mother, who had lived to seventy-two as a quite contented, generally incoherent lush. And then the suicide, which seemed extravagant. Her life was a mess, granted—but more so than anyone else's? To do it during Christmas had seemed so stagy—or had she been, quite genuinely, unaware of the season? What implication could Christmas have for a woman living alone and, for all intents and purposes, liking it? Still, he stared at the date as though the black, precise letters would serve up some key or illumination.

"Darling?"

It was Ginny, fresh from an orgy of shopping, eyes bright. "Are you almost done?"

"I haven't really begun," he said.

His wife had the illusion that he was always at work on some project of earthshaking significance—or so she seemed to pretend.

"Because, well, I told the Murgitraughs we'd meet them at two."

"The who?"

"You remember, he did that portrait of Sean Olsen's wife. I had thought he might do Mandy. He's awfully talented."

"Umm." A vision of his stepdaughter, immortalized for the ages in some ten-by-twelve oily masterpiece, hanging over the nonexistent fireplace.

"So, anyway, if you're going to change. I mean, it isn't formal, but—"

"Where are we meeting them?"

"At the Whitney . . . They have some new things, Gwen said."

"Gwen?"

"His wife. You remember. The tall blonde?"

He didn't. She flashed him a smile. "I'll just wash up."

"Right."

Not that he was especially loathe to be torn from the exams. "Is Mandy coming?" he called in to the bedroom. Their

bedroom was on the ground floor, Mandy's was on the upper
floor of the duplex apartment that was paid for out of his
wife's ample inheritance of stocks.

"Why should *Mandy* go?" Ginny had the curious notion
he "encouraged" Mandy in her furtive passion for himself. At
first when they had married she had gone around beaming to
friends over the change in her until-then hostile little daughter. "She's just like a girl in love," she had chortled to Esther
and Pam and the rest of them. And then, naturally enough,
the tide had turned and revealed the murky depths below.

Ginny was in the bath. He "surprised" her there, submerged in sudsy water, a large bouffant cap on her head. She
smiled up at him. It was vaguely reminiscent of various
Grade B movies he had seen and had been bored by. Should
he plunge his arms into the scalding water up to the elbow,
seize her in his arms, and cry . . . Yet Max pitied his wife,
pitied her for the pleasant, attractive, but undeniably middle-aged face that hovered between a smile and something
sadder as she soaked in fragrant oils for his sake or, hopefully,
for some nonexistent lover. He pitied his wife, yes, but in the
sense that he pitied a dog with a rash on its behind, the pity
never quite diffusing into genuine compassion. She had made
her bed, she was lying in it. If not him, there would have
been another bloodsucker, possibly worse, more pernicious.
His sins were overt, uncomplicated ones. And—he prided
himself on this point—he had never lied to her. He had said,
"I'm marrying you for your money. I'm sick of poverty," and
she had honored his refreshing candor.

Everyone had been glad at that time—his sisters with their
large, respectable suburban families, grown, in their forties,
so alike he scarcely distinguished them anymore, his brother,
his parents still venerably alive and active. Everyone was glad
that he had chosen a woman of his own age. Or so it was
discreetly said. Not some wretched teenybopper to foul up

the family nest, nothing at all way out, but instead a woman who, like him, had "been through a lot." So she was rich. It couldn't hurt, could it?

"It's funny you don't remember the Murgitraughs," Ginny said, toweling herself off.

"Should I? Were they distinctive in some way?"

"Yes! Well, I mean, he's very . . . unusual and she's very . . . beautiful."

Unusual might mean the man was a raving madman, and *beautiful?* Well, that could be the simple truth. His wife had an accurate and unbiased eye for the attractions of her potential rivals.

"She's very tall," she said. "Oh, six feet maybe."

"Good God."

"A very handsome woman."

So she was. Gwendolyn Murgitraugh, standing by her husband's side, all of six feet at least, was a predictable but stunning combination of cheekbones, elaborate hair, gigantic eyes, a breathy English accent that made her sound as though she'd just run around the block several times.

"I knew your wife at Smith," she breathed to him as his wife and Jim, the eccentric but successful portrait painter, were examining some paintings up close.

"Did you?" Should he say, Which one?

"She was an extraordinary person."

"Ginny went to Radcliffe."

She smiled secretively. "Alice."

"Oh, Alice."

Gwendolyn Murgitraugh was fixing him with an uncomfortably intense, knowing look. "Alice and I were very close at one time . . ." Pause. "I was devastated to learn of her death."

The sculpture in the foreground at which his present wife and Gwendolyn M's present husband were staring was a jagged slash of metal, twisted into an X shape. Staring at it, Max permitted himself the luxury of hating this woman by his side, a comparative stranger, with the casual insinuation of her prattle about death. But of course she must have tried it too. Sleeping pills, this or that. Before she'd met Jim, between lovers. When the eighty thousand dollars or whatever she was earning as a model "wasn't enough." "How did you learn of her death?" he said.

"I read of it in the paper . . . But you were divorced then, weren't you?"

"Yes."

"Strange her doing it like that, with the plastic bag and the—"

"How did you hear of that?" The paper had printed "natural causes," which in a sense was true enough.

"From a friend . . . Henry Trent."

But he would not permit himself to be drawn further into this. Because Henry Trent, whom at one point he had hated—the first and, as it turned out, most respectable of Alice's lovers—was as unimportant to him now as that guard standing in the corner, looking with boredom at the giant Wesselman nude on the opposite wall. Because his whole former life, when he thought about it at all, seemed as remote as though he had never lived it at all but merely read of it in some book as a schoolboy. The person he was then—he had been a virgin when he had married Alice, she had worn her black hair parted in the middle, their naïveté, both of them with their asthma and their families and their ambitions for each other and their life together—was something in which he no longer believed, even in retrospect.

"I haven't seen Henry Trent in a long time," he said. "How is he?"

"Well, not so well, really." You could see she devoured and loved these mournful details. "Those ulcers, and then, Carolyn hasn't been well."

Wasn't his wife dead yet? Hadn't she had cancer supposedly? Which in some incredible way was supposed to justify his adulteries.

"I thought she'd be dead by now," he remarked as they passed on to the next room.

"Well, they've removed just about *all* of her. But she goes on living."

"Remarkable."

"It is, isn't it? . . . Poor Henry has been through such a lot."

Suddenly Ginny beckoned. "Come here, you two! What are you gossiping about?"

"Old friends," Gwendolyn Murgitraugh said, with a smile at Max. "We know some people in common."

"It's *you* I'd like to do, Virginia sweetheart," Jim Murgitraugh was saying, grinning wildly at Ginny as she politely accepted a drink from him.

Is he for real? Max was thinking, slouched back in the couch, with that wild head of blondish curls and his wooden beads—one part hippy, one part gay, nine parts phony. He has a Jewish mother in the Bronx, no doubt, to whom he's little Bubela.

"Do you play an instrument?" Jim was saying.

"Me? No, I—" Ginny blushed. Even now, at forty-five, with two bad marriages behind her and a third one going bad, she had that odd innocent blush that was so genuine and made her look so vulnerable, both calling attention to her age and defying it, that Max, watching it, often felt an inward cringe. "I've never had an ear for music," she said. "My sisters all took piano and—"

"Because I see you, somehow—" eyes shut, dreamy—"with a cello—"

"*Playing* a cello?"

"Playing, maybe just holding it . . . You know, I love the tones of a cello—I mean the color tones—that rich red brown, like your hair. I'd see it all in those shades, like one of those old photographs, mellow—"

"Mandy has red hair," Ginny said nervously.

"Does she? Yes, of course, I recall—"

The doorbell rang. Another couple. Introductions. Shortly later a few more. The noise quotient rose. More smoke. Max, who had given up smoking, began wandering restlessly around the oversized living room. How long was this to go on? Dinner too? Outside it was black as pitch.

"Do you like our house?" It was Gwendolyn, changed, at what point he couldn't recall, into a splashy purple and yellow Oriental print. Trousers? A skirt? It was hard to tell.

"Lovely."

"Jim all but designed it . . . Ripped down walls. He had this concept—"

In the background a discussion was ensuing about some pot brought to the gathering by a stoutish man in a goatee. "Great stuff," he was saying.

Ginny was always enthusiastic about pot. Part of the letting-go bit, though until now she'd only gotten mild highs and had been very disappointed. He saw her intently watching the goateed man.

"Let me show you the rest of the house."

Blindly, tired, he followed her.

It seemed it was a duplex also. Gwendolyn M, like himself, had married into a duplex. Well, there were worse things to marry into. For some reason hard to fathom, the kitchen was on the top floor, a giant room, dazzling with pots and chrome fixtures. "Jim is a great cook."

Jim's talents seemed endless. "And what do *you* do?" he said.

She looked at him.

"Your husband's abilities seem so diversified."

"Oh no, it's just—" She looked defensive. "He really *is* good at all those things. He's not gay or anything."

"I didn't assume—"

"Well, some people do. You know. I mean, his looks—"

"That's just part of the scene."

"Right!" She was relieved he understood. "When I met him, he was just a boy from the Bronx, a real square. Now he's loosened up a little. His analyst says that—"

She flung open another door. It was a narrow room with rows upon rows of cans in all sizes, rather like a giant Pop painting with all the bright labels glaring out. "The pantry," she said.

She evidently intended to be seduced in one of these many rooms. From the vague glaze that came over her expression, Max gathered this was the one. The "scene" downstairs was too uninviting for him to resist her. Besides, though he had screwed women he disliked before, toward none could he remember such a pure, unadulterated (pun?) hatred as toward Gwendolyn Murgitraugh, with her insect eyelashes and pouty English mouth. The very purity of his feeling was so sharp as to lend the moment of their coupling, otherwise undistinguished, a certain memorable quality. As for Gwendolyn, she was agile and professionally adept, as though there were another customer waiting outside the door. Even her cry of passion from the pseudo-Spanish linoleum floor seemed to him rehearsed, as though, in daily voice lessons, she had practiced to attain the right pitch and tone.

When they were done, she withdrew, from behind a box of Aunt Jemima pancakes, a box of flowered Kleenex. Was this a regular routine? The pantry somehow aphrodisiac with its brightly colored labels?

"Why'd you marry Ginny?" Loose, slurred, her speech acquired the vulgarity he had sensed all along behind the acquired upper-class Englishness.

"Why not?"

"I'd have thought you went for—women of quality."

"Nope . . . I have catholic tastes."

She looked puzzled, evidently wondering if she should take this personally, then deciding to pass it by. "Don't you have a type or anything? I mean, Alice and Ginny are so different. Were." She stumbled over the tense.

"Are and were."

"Most people pick similar mates."

A truism? "Was the former Mr. Murgitraugh like the present one?" A sheer guess. Correct as it turned out.

"Well, no, but Gene—we were very young."

He didn't want reminiscenses of the early life and loves of G.M. "Jim's a swinger."

"Oh, not really . . . He's serious. Just because he's a success doesn't mean—"

"Far be it from me to sneer at success."

But she was melancholy, distracted by memories of Lonesome Gene. "He's married now. Has two kids. Sends me pictures sometimes."

"Cute little buggers?"

Gwendolyn smiled dreamily. "They are . . . really."

"So, have a couple."

"I can't."

"Oh?"

Rushing on, frantic. "I'd adopt one. I've love a little black baby . . . Or a Vietnamese one . . . But Jim doesn't. He feels—"

"Oh, of course."

"I would die for a little baby," Gwendolyn Murgitraugh said, closing her eyes as though in orgasm.

Why were people's lives destroyed in such simple ways? *A wants an apple but gets a banana. B wants . . .* He rose. "Come on, Gwennie . . . We better move."

She looked startled. "Gene used to call me that."

"Sorry."

"No, I like it."

So, he was being deprived of what had seemed the most genuine emotion he was likely to feel that evening—hatred. He was disappointed. Beneath the phony exterior of a Gwendolyn M beats the heart of a . . .

Her hand rested on a can of Campbells baked beans. "When I was at Smith, I admired Alice so much . . . I wanted to *be* her . . . She seemed to know just what she wanted out of life."

"She didn't."

"Her father used to come up and speak . . . Such a handsome man. Some of the girls had crushes on him . . . I never even *knew* my father."

"Shouldn't we go down?"

She was in a reverie. Maybe she'd had a little pot before. "Alice wrote poetry . . . She did *everything* . . . You know something?"

"What?"

"I made a pass at Alice's father once. He was so distinguished. He came to this party. He'd just lectured on—oh, I forget what. But Alice gave this party for him . . . I think we would've—only it was inconvenient."

"I'm sure he would have."

"He had a moustache . . . I didn't used to like men with moustaches. But on him it was different."

"Let's go down, Gwennie."

She was angry. "We'll go down, we'll go down. What's the big rush?"

"No rush."

"See them all vomiting over each other. What's there to see?"

"Nothing." But he remained poised near the door.

She sprang up, pulling her swirls of Oriental silk around

her. "What I can't figure out is, how come Alice married someone like you?" The hostility, if such it was, seemed so ingenuous it almost cleared the air.

"I don't know."

"Her father was so famous . . . I thought she'd marry some *famous* person."

"So did she."

"Maybe she thought *you'd* be famous, huh?"

"Maybe."

"Well . . ." Indifferent now. "You never know what you're marrying."

Ginny appeared to have had several small but intense visions that in the car on the way home she tried to convey to him. He listened and did not listen.

"How'd it go with Gwen?" she said suddenly.

"Okay."

"Nothing special?"

"No . . . She likes to do it in the pantry."

"She looked a little ill when you came down."

"I felt a little ill."

"Poor old thing. You're too much of a gentleman."

"Old-time chivalry."

She had the key. Max walked past her into the pleasantly crowded living room. This is a nice house. How does he afford it on a high school teacher's salary? Well, he has a talent for picking wives. You see, the first one had a famous father. And the second one had a lot of money.

"Max!"

The sound from the other end of the house was like a screech. "It's Timmy!"

"What about him?"

"The school called. He tried to run away."

"Where to?"

"I don't know. He's okay, though."

Mandy, in flowered pajamas, was puffy with tears. "They said—they'd call back."

But the call, an hour later, revealed nothing beyond the fact that he was back in the dorm, had been caught "near the state line." More talk about "emotional upset," "adjusting to the strains of a broken home." Blah and more blah.

"That school is *crap*," Ginny said violently, drinking black coffee in the kitchen, ravenously picking at Chinese noodles left over from a take-out dinner. "We've *got* to take him out of it."

"Where to?"

"Thare are places . . . Let him stay home."

"He doesn't want to." His words had been: "This isn't my home."

"Maybe he's changed."

"Maybe."

The next morning he would set off for the school. Yet even now Max knew how he would feel. Not ready. Not ready for a six-hour drive, confrontations with headmasters and school psychologists, not ready most of all for Timmy, who would say, "Look Dad, lay *off*," who would be angry and hostile and not say why he had tried to do it, who would stare at him with the eyes of his dead first wife who had married the wrong man and only in death corrected her mistake.